As
Malcriadas
or Names We Inherit

Carlo Matos

As
Malcriadas
or Names We Inherit

All rights reserved. Published by New Meridian, part of the non-profit organization New Meridian Arts, 2022.

LIBRARY OF CONGRESS CATALOGING-IN-PUBLICATION DATA

As Malcriadas, or Names We Inherit
Authored by Carlo Matos

ISBN: 9781737249153
LCCN: 2021950896

Acknowledgments

Selections from this manuscript have appeared in the *Bad Jobs and Bullshit* anthology (Geeky Press, 2016) and a few moments have been reimagined from *The Quitters* (Tortoise Books, 2017).

The author would like to thank the La Romita School of Art, Sundress Academy for the Arts, and Disquiet International Literary Program for the time and support to complete this manuscript. Thanks also go out to Jackie Wright and Michael Colson for reading early drafts of the manuscript and providing valuable feedback. Carlo would also like to thank his partner, Heather Leigh, for all the emotional support during the writing of this manuscript.

For all the malcriadas:
the insolent, the crude, the ill-bred;
may you never change

For Blair's Carriage

For Gauge

For Tempus Fugit

Contents

"Dei-te o nome de José para te dar um nome que te servisse ao mesmo tempo de alma. E tu—como saber jamais que nome me deste?"

—CLARICE LISPECTOR,
The Crime of the Mathematics Professor

"Names have a talismanic quality in the United States. We are a nation of Gatsbys, die hard believers in the magical powers of personal reinvention. Change the name and change the past … create a phantom being that exists only in the present and future tense."

—NATHAN RABIN, *The Big Rewind*

"How did you hold her? Was it? Like this? And when you kissed her? Like this?"

—SANDRA CISNEROS, *The House on Mango Street*

Preface

BY AMY SAYRE BAPTISTA, AUTHOR OF PRIMITIVITY

In *As Malcriadas*, Carlo Matos shows himself to be a triple threat. His prose sings and soars right alongside his previous award winning playwrighting and poetry. From the first lines to the concluding, *As Malcriadas* feeds the reader a lyrical prose, "My mouth is water but not a body I want to drown in—a body that buries what I thought to share. It is a breath from below that cracks a road that isn't water but still holds the memory of you like rivers are said to do."

We meet a cast of characters, four self-titled misfits, whose story is a kind of sharp-edged saudade, nostalgic yet never indulgently so. Manny, Em, Gomez, and Gilga are a Gen X tapestry and Matos a master weaver. Their narrative follows the heroic journey that the youth in all of us hungers for. Questioning time and memory, the story moves back and forth from grunge era to a near present. By extension the reader is inevitably confronted with asking what might have been, and further, what is the value of even asking?

With focus on the absolute loyalty of lifelong friends and sometimes lovers, this novel relentlessly examines what happens when we are forced to admit we can never fully know the people closest to us. Expect four characters finding themselves a life path that does not offer any shortcuts. These are the children of blue collar, Portuguese immigrants trying to break out of a town where millwork and stoic resignation deny the promises of the new world. If you think you know this story, hold off, these characters are bold, sexually awake and searching. But the real magic is that while the experience is unique to these four, it is universal to readers.

The concept of naming resounds large in *As Malcriadas* and readers are asked to consider if we name others with our own dysfunction, unhappiness, and failure. This novel begins with swords in the dark and brings us back to that sharp point by the close. Be warned, Matos's muscular prose jabs, parries, and feints as it is unbelievably flexible in its construction, spinning out questions that sting when answered. And reader, true to its Gen X setting, it hurts so good.

EM DASH

1

Three knocks on a metal door, a magic number, a code, like how mysteries begin: a knock, a darkened room; three shaded figures enter. They are on time, at least, which is a good sign. Timely people can be trusted. They plan and execute, aren't haphazard or impulsive by nature. I have been planning this night for a very long time and the only thing that worries me now is the possibility that this dude and his buddies will chicken out, fearing all the things left undone, of being spared the learning curve. People always promise more than they can deliver, and the disappointment never gets any easier to accept. "I'm sorry," they'll say. "I'm sorry." But I'm sorry doesn't pay the bills or underwrite the business of adulthood. I wish I was someone who didn't keep score, wish I could grow out of allegory and become more than a lesson to be learned, more than a return to cruelty. Three men enter and everything skews awkward rather than mysterious—junior-high-dance awkward. Three men, unsure of what to say or where to look, come face-to-face with three women standing almost at attention. We two-step like nervous beginning actors. One of the men readies himself to speak. "No names," I remind him before he blows the whole thing in the exact first moment.

The basement, its moldy concrete and spiders, is lit by a few naked lightbulbs—house centipedes skittering out of the corners of our eyes. I had never even seen one until I moved to Chicago; now, they are ubiquitous like the sulfur smell coming from a nearby drain, always more oppressive during rain storms. It must be raining somewhere in the city. In Chicago, even the rain can kill, like a boat to a reef, which is beautiful when left alone but a disaster when the two meet. Let this not be a disaster or, at the very least, let it be beautiful. Let it be something. This building belongs to my friend. I told her we needed it for band practice. I'm not in a band, though I played bass in one when I was in high school—something almost beyond believing now. The top light casts shadows convincing enough to make even the cheesiest movie dialogue possible. This could be a drug deal, has the tone of a meeting of spies, a conspiracy taking its first unsure steps. It could be the moment in a revenge drama before the trap is sprung, having been held in tension during a book-length flashback. It could be the breaking of sexual taboos so epiphanic in movies but banal in real life. It could be, but it isn't.

"Terms of engagement?"

The one I call Athos looks wide-eyed at his friends and I realize he may not have thought everything through, after all. This whole thing could still come crashing down.

"I don't know," he says looking to me for an answer. I do not provide one. "First blood?" he finally suggests and shrugs, like a child admitting what he wants to a group of adults who will most assuredly make fun of any answer he might suggest.

"Historically considered unmanly."

"Well, what do you suggest? To the death?" he says jokingly before a worried look he fails to hide washes over his face.

"We go until one of us quits. Only way I can be satisfied."

"Or a second calls it off," says his friend, Porthos or maybe Aramis.

"Have it your way," Athos says, catching my *Princess Bride* reference.

"Terms accepted."

We shake hands, the formalities of ritual almost as important as the act itself—almost. I remind everyone there will be no phones and no filming during the duel. Everyone nods. When I say the word "duel," it sticks a little to the roof of my mouth, but that's what it is, a duel: incontrovertible, simple, true.

His seconds help him with his doublet, the kind made for sparring. It's thicker than a piece of stage costume, thick enough for running drills or for competition but will be less than useless against the point of a blade. He slips on his long leather gloves—the kind people in movies are always slapping each other with—and takes a few swipes with his rapier. These swords, it must be noted, are nothing like the foils my friends and I stole from gym class when we were in high school and still high on *The Three Musketeers*, the one featuring the musical ménage à trois with Sting, Rod Stewart, and Bryan Adams. We Frankensteined it all the way to my best friend's house, a foil tucked each into a pant leg, still young enough for foolishness to be more than an exercise in how wrong one can be.

I warm up with some practice lunges with my Spanish cup hilt style rapier, what my people probably would have carried in the Iberian Peninsula, though it isn't very likely anyone in the long peasant line of my Portuguese family would have had the cash to own a sword or the training to use it. It is clear Athos knows what he is doing; he is not a person who thinks he can learn to fence by watching *Zorro* nor is he one of those *Highlander* geeks who dream of becoming immortals by battling it out in their backyards with modified hockey sticks and baseball helmets. He has studied. In swordplay, as in most important things, really knowing what you're doing can be the difference between life and death. In this situation, ignorance will get you immediate, concrete, and conclusive results—and some part of me feels great relief in that idea.

"This is pretty fucked up," I hear Porthos, or was it Aramis, whisper too loud.

"Then why did you come?" says Athos matching his pitch.

"I don't know. I wanted to see if it was for real."

"Well, it is, so can you just shut up, please?"

These swords have been sharpened, but we are wearing steel helmets and gorgets to protect our faces and necks. The goal is not necessarily to kill one another, though the chance of someone dying is definitely real. A helmet isn't going to protect you from a lunge to the heart or the guts. This is no game and what matters actually matters and it matters right now.

One of my seconds marks twenty paces and we toe the line. "*Salute,*" she says in Italian, and we salute. The sword is steady in my hand, though I feel a muscle twitch deep inside my body, as if my hand knows better than to tremble in this moment. "*In guardia,*" and we get into our stances. My shoulders are nearly in profile, weight way back on the rear leg. Athos's weight is forward, his body crouched with shoulders square and his butt scooted so far out it looks like a comical exaggeration of a courtly bow. This is Fabris's guard. I have experimented with it but prefer the modified Capo Ferro guard my instructor teaches better. There is something that just makes cold hard sense to me about leaning as far away as possible from the point of a blade rather than towards it like Athos is doing, though his stance provides him other advantages.

"Pronti. A voi!" my second says, and moves quickly out of the way like the scantily-clad girls do in all those car racing movies. I inch towards him slowly, heel-to-toe. He waits patiently, changing the angle of his sword depending on which line I am trying to control. He is tall, so I must be very careful of his reach. In rapier fighting, reach is everything. I have to control distance perfectly or it'll be over before it starts. I test a lunge, but he takes a half step back, anticipating the attack and keeping safely out of range. He is trying to judge my timing. At this point, we remain in thrall to the taboo of steel, by the fact of blood, by the unmistakable integrity of skin. The boiler kicks on impatiently and water screams through the old pipes with determination and purpose. Sweat runs down my back following the river of my spine and soaking the heavy sail cloth of my jacket. There is still time to stop this thing from happening and the thought makes me so anxious I feint as if to attack, and, this time, Athos bites. He attempts to meet my forward step with a counter lunge, but instead of lunging forward, I sweep my front leg back and shift into a high guard, changing the angle of the sword like a picador in a bullfight and bringing the point down into the meat of his shoulder. It goes in with only slight resistance, soft like a marshmallow steaked for the fire. His sword, on the other hand, falls safely short of my abdomen. I have used this move often in sparring. Once you land it on someone, it will not work again, but this is the key difference between sparring and dueling. The true nature of sparring is repetition, refinement. The true nature of dueling is efficiency—that or brute force.

The effect is instantaneous. Calling it a jolt doesn't quite do it justice, though an electrical metaphor seems appropriate judging by the way Athos's body stiffens. His body can't seem to come to grips with what has just happened to it, like when you stub a toe on the coffee table or bang an elbow on a door knob—the kind of pain that seems to require only that you wait for it to pass though it feels in the moment like it never will. When the pain subsides enough, he swipes at his shoulder and, sure enough, there is blood on his glove, making the black leather slick and blacker still. For a moment, we appear stunned, comically confused by our surprise because we knew blood would be there. In fact, this is the very reason we have come in the first place. And what I want to do most now is laugh in that inappropriate but nearly unquenchable way one wants to laugh at a funeral though nothing is remotely funny, in that nervous way confusion comes to interrupt moments that should be of great consequence and yet fall sadly short. We all fall for failure with our eyes wide open, no matter what we say later. It dreads to us even in the most banal moments of our lives yet falls short in the ones of dire consequence.

A constricted part of me relaxes for a moment. I'd just stabbed a person in real life. More precisely, I'd just stabbed a human being in a duel and civilization had not come crashing down around my ears. The relief that comes from overcoming the fear that things will not happen is intense but it is also brief, like having the hangman's rope shot out from above you before you run out of air, like in those old westerns my avó used to love: *A Fistful of Dollars, A Few Dollars More, The Good, The Bad and the Ugly.*

"Take a moment."

"No," he says, grimly, knowing a break in the action will not help him. He toes the line bravely and we face off again. He tries to shake some life into his dead hand, but the strength will not return. When we reengage, I lunge and beat his parry easily and the point of my sword pierces the same shoulder, much deeper this time, but he doesn't cry out, as if being stung once has solved the mystery of steel. How easily we adapt, the great strength and curse of our species. The sword falls limply to the ground and clangs, the steel artlessly marking the moment.

He reaches one more time for his sword, gets to his feet, tries but fails to lift it. "I'm done," he says. His seconds rush to his aid, and I walk over to thank him, his upper lip pale and lined with drops of sweat. "That was awesome," he says one word at a time, wonder or something like it in each syllable, as if he could sleep here, as if something had been done and done well. The feeling I had a moment ago is already vanishing, escaping in the return to my private body. When you don't belong anywhere, you make yourself the locus of all things, but the second you do, you realize it isn't somewhere you want to be from. What could have fallen short? I had just stabbed a human being—twice—pierced his body and drew blood. I had traded steel and risked death and murder, and yet there isn't a mark on me, nothing to prove I had swung from the gallows, however briefly, and survived.

FROST HEAVES EMMANUEL

2

Roller Derby made a dramatic resurgence at the turn of the twenty-first century. In the 1930s, it was a legitimate coed sport that could sell out Madison Square Garden, but by century's end, it had slowly devolved—at least in one extreme iteration— into a scripted, WWE-style spectacle starring the likes of the dastardly Violators and their rivals, the heroic L.A. T-Birds. And when the ratings bottomed out, the sport nearly disappeared. However, in 2001, a group of enterprising women in Austin, Texas brought the sport back from near oblivion. Unlike the original, these new derby leagues are run by skaters, for skaters, and, at least in its current manifestation, have a decidedly feminist, underground, DIY, punk-rock aesthetic. Most importantly—and this is not to be underestimated—anyone can play if they can meet minimum skating requirements.

Tonight, the pressure is really on because this bout is historic, at least as far as Chicago roller derby is concerned. It is the long-awaited, much anticipated, oft-debated, much belated, cross-town classic, which has been years in the making. There were several close calls, but the bout never seemed to materialize. It looked like Chicago's two premier flat track roller derby teams would never face off against one another. The Chicago Red Hots, the team Em plays for, are in for a tough one. The Windy City Rollers, though diminished over the last few years, are still a much better team. But no one beats the Red Hots' jeerleaders, who come gunned to the teeth with posters declaring WCR loves Fox News; WCR listens to Nickelback, and WCR reads Dan Brown. These are fierce women, but sometimes ferocity isn't enough.

The bout starts close, very close, much closer than anticipated. The first fifteen minutes are intense as each team fights bitterly over each little advantage, grinding for control of every inch of territory. Graceful skaters chosen for their dexterity glide as if riding gentle winds between the shifting continents of the enormous defensive skaters, chosen for their raw power and toughness. Smaller and speedier skaters scorch the track, counting on their quickness and reflexes to make it beyond the reefs to safer waters. For a short time, it looks like the game is going to be really competitive, but if you look closely you can see the Red Hots starting to wear. Keeping up with the well-oiled machine that is the Windy City Rollers is taking its toll, and cracks are starting to show in their defense. WCR starts putting up points that go unanswered. The Red Hots' aggressive and reckless barbarian style comes with a huge energy bill, and they begin slowly losing ground to the precision and tactical awareness of the more polished team.

By half time, WCR has totally figured them out and have a commanding fifty-point lead. By this point, the game is no longer competitive; however, it is an opportunity for both teams to try out some of their less-experienced players in the jamming position. In derby, the jammers are the stars of the show; they literally wear a starred panty over their helmets. The jammers are the ones who score the points, the derby equivalent of the quarterback. Everyone wants to be the jammer, until they hit the track, that is. Once on the line, at the rear of that many-headed and many-wheeled hydra called the pack, revelations come unbidden—revelations foretelling immediate and very real doom. The disparity in score, however, hardly daunts the Red Hots' jeering section, which remains loud and enthusiastic till the bitter and predictable end. With the new jammers coming to the line, I have something to keep my mind on the game. Unlike the teen spirit crowd—the ones who go to sporting events in order to drink beer and confront a fictional adversary, who pretend to draw a line in the sand with a proverbial broad sword as a horde of barbarian riders storm towards the wooden gates of their imaginary village—I am here to watch strategy and talent match wits, and to gnaw my nails to the quick watching Em dash around the track.

There are two new faces up at the line for the Red Hots who are low on the roster. They are really members of the B team. Most derby teams have several rosters from which to stock their A team. Em Dash, one of my oldest friends, is one of these skaters. I hesitate at the word "friend" because I am not sure one can consider it friendship if it is completely one-sided and anonymous. Are we friends if we haven't spoken in years? Does Em love me like I love her, like I have always loved her? How does she love? Is it, like this? Like a murmur in passing? Like a book on a shelf? Like the dead? We had met when we were four years old and were best friends before that first day was out. For the next 15 years, nothing came between us; not a single person mattered the way we mattered to each other. Until college! I guess I should be satisfied. Most marriages don't make it that far. But like many marriages, I assume, one day it is simply over. There is no thunder, no wind, no smell of ozone. And like married couples, the "why" is only clear to one of the parties—and that isn't me. Anyone who says it was "mutual" is probably lying or is the party trying to assuage their own guilt for leaving, if guilt is what it is. It may not be. We started one day as friends and by the end of that day in 1996—almost twenty years ago—we weren't anymore. Em dumped me, and I was lost. I am lost. I will be lost. Who knows what tense to be lost in.

Em doesn't know I've seen every single bout this season. We lost track in college and it was only the biggest of flukes that allowed me to find her again because she made the mistake of using the same nickname we gave her in high school as her derby name: Em Dash. How many times in life has a name become a destiny, given shape to what was otherwise randomness and chaos, like Adam who gave the animals names but not souls, or so we are led to believe? I had given Em that name. Our 10th grade English teacher once suggested she use em dashes instead of so many commas, and Em asked incredulously, "What is an em dash?" I responded without even thinking, "You're an em dash," and the whole class laughed. To this day, I have no idea what the hell that was supposed to mean, but, like many a good nickname, the reason why one sticks and another does not is mysterious at best—a shape hidden deep in the math. The conditions for a nickname are as baroque and finicky as an alchemical process. One must take into consideration the phase of the moon, barometric pressure, the presence of solar flares or sun spots, planetary wobble, and the gravitational influence of the nearest super black hole—among many other things. This is why you cannot simply give yourself a nickname. Em must have figured it would be unlikely that anyone from our little east coast town would also end up in Chicago. Most never left the place. She figured wrong.

When her turn arrives, Em takes the line. I've seen her jam before but never against such an overwhelming force. I am genuinely concerned that she may be out of her depth and that is when people get hurt. The whistle blows and she takes off, and then just as quickly she is down. She gets back to her feet and comes at the pack again, only to be knocked to her knees a second time. WCR's blockers are suffocating, but Em does not wilt under the pressure. She hammers away, never allowing futility to dissuade her, and how loud it whispers in moments like this one. She does not manage to score a single point when the opposing jammer calls off the jam, making the iconic gesture of hands touching the waist and then flashing upward like an aircraft marshaller. Em returns to the bench, exhausted but undaunted. Hermione Danger takes the line next and doesn't have much better luck. WCR is without mercy. They do not care about the gulf in the score. It isn't about winning; a message is being sent. A few jams later and Em is back on the line. The whistle blows and WCR's Agatha Crushdie, who had been all over Em in the previous jam, nails her to the floor before Em manages to complete more than a couple full strides. The pack is moving at a good clip and Em gets to her feet as quickly as she can, though she appears to be slowing down. Having to pick yourself up over and over is very tiring. On her feet again, the pack sailing away, she begins to build a head of steam trying to catch up, but rather than looking for holes in the defense, she begins tracking Agatha Crushdie like a MiG-28 closing in on the much-larger F-14A Tomcat. The pack looms like a tidal wave closer to my spot in the crowd when Em collides at full speed with Agatha Crush-die, who manages somehow to deflect the full force of Em's blow right back at her with a move called a can opener. Em shoots off the track like a rock at the end of a sling, barely missing the diehard fans sitting at the edge of the track in the aptly-named "suicide seats" and crashes into the first couple rows of chairs directly in front of where I am standing. I could hide, but I don't. I could rush to her side, but I don't. I could vanish before she sees me … I could … but I don't.

The people in the audience help her to her feet as the pack drifts away again, leaving Em behind, a castaway thrown overboard into the sea. Em regains her legs and locks eyes with me. She holds my stare for what seems like a moment too long and then skates back onto the track to hunt for the pack once more, hoping to score some points before the jam is called off. "Did she see me?" Twenty years is a long time. This could be a reunion. It could be the start of something. It could be a resolution, but it isn't. What I would have given for a smile or even a nod. I would have taken a nod. I would have taken a knee, like derby girls do when someone goes down but does not get up. I would have given anything.

THE GREAT GILGAMESH

3

SOMERSET 1995

"He has one job, one! Keep the damn beat. How hard is that?" I think for the millionth time since this drummer joined the band, the thought so loud in my head it nearly overpowers the sheer volume of my Marshall half stack, which I have cranked to earsplitting volumes to drown out the lousy rhythm section. The drummer—I refuse to call him "our" drummer—came in half a beat late and ruined the opening of a song that starts on a very pronounced and obvious downbeat, a song we had rehearsed over and over all week. I have to literally bite my cheek so that I don't smash him upside the head with my crappy yard-sale Stratocaster. It would be no great loss to drummers or guitars everywhere had I used my axe to cleave him in twain. It's like one of those clocks that are always behind. Better to just take a hammer to the thing and resign yourself to sundials and obelisks.

Ever since our original drummer left the band, we have been trapped in an endless rotation of drummers. The drummer conundrum, as it is called in learned circles, is a known problem. Either the drummers are good, which means they play in a million bands and are, therefore, never available for practice or gigs, or they are terrible and are hardly worth the effort. Drummers belong to everyone and no one. Our current drummer has no rhythm whatsoever, but he does have a van so we let him stay in the band. Forget about talent. Forget about originality. Forget personality. This guy can't play a copper pot and a wooden spoon. And he isn't by any stretch of the imagination the worst of the hideous bunch we auditioned for the spot. One guy was always late for rehearsal. And I do not mean five or ten minutes, which is already an offense worthy of defenestration or amputation of favored limbs as far as I am concerned; he would be hours late and sometimes just wouldn't show up at all. Another guy couldn't "remember" the songs. That one is still rattling around in my head, finding no clear exit, doing damage to every thought in its vicinity. All I wanted to do was write songs, do something serious, so why do I get stuck with calling the delinquent drummer? Why do I have to interrupt rehearsal to teach the forgetful one the songs again and again while everyone else goes outside to smoke cigarettes and finish off the fake cappuccino powder we all loved? And those were my cigarettes! Fuckers! It seriously makes me wonder about the nature of the universe when a drummer can't keep time. As far as I am concerned, it is THE thing that separates humanity from the beasts of the field. We took our first steps out of the haze of ancient cave fire when our hominid ancestress made her first appointment. "Meet me at the big rock when the stars are in such and such a place in the sky," she said, and bam! Civilization.

When our original drummer played, it didn't sound like marching band music. Listen to the rhythm section of most rock songs; it sounds like John Philip Sousa. John Fucking Philip Sousa! It is not something you want to be aware of, but once you have the thought, it is unstoppable. One day it's teen rebellion and mosh pits and the next it's marching in synch and baton twirling. Take away the flannel and the distortion and replace with polyester and euphonium and you got yourself a parade. To be fair, I actually liked the euphonium. It had to put up with the haughty attitude of the trombones and the working-man's solidity of the tubas, but at least it wasn't the freak in the family. That honor fell to the aptly named Sousaphone, named after the one Portuguese guy to make a name for himself in a country that knew literally nothing of our people nor cared to know. John Philip Sousa and Emeril Lagasse. BAM, indeed.

"You're making your John Philip Sousa face," mouths Em and Manny laughs. Manny and Em are my best friends since elementary school and don't need to actually hear words to know what I am thinking.

"He was off the damn beat again."

"I know," says Manny and hits the nearest cymbal with the head of his guitar. Someone needs to be on the beat, so he might as well keep hitting it all night long.

If you are in the audience, you can tell the song is coming to an end because Ash—our lead singer—is doing his Eddie Vedder "so-he-chases-them-away" invisible-force-hand-thing. It is one of his stock-in-trade imitations. It never varies. When the song finally ends, Em says into her mic, "John Philip Sousa, ladies and gentlemen, John Philip Sousa," and once again I am reminded of how much I love her. She's Tori Amos's dawn red hair and bitten lip; she's one leg up on the keyboard; she's "where the drifts get deeper." Em is a beach at night and all the ocean's water and just as impossible.

Senior year is almost over. This will most likely be our last gig before we all leave for college. It will certainly be our last gig at the high school. We had been invited to headline this benefit concert for a student who had been killed by a drunk driver earlier in the year. A drunk driver nailed him as he was walking home from track practice. The thing about this dumb, small suburb we couldn't wait to get away from is that it is predictably insulated, protected in certain important ways. He was the first kid any of us knew who'd died. We had never known a young person to die, not in the small sphere of our private lives. I didn't know him, but I have a particular hatred of drunk drivers. Maybe if I hadn't been nearly killed by one when I was 12, I too would have the cavalier attitude towards drinking and driving so common among people young and old. No one loves a drunk driver seems axiomatic but that doesn't seem to stop people from becoming them. A monster is as a monster does. Monsters are made, born in the aftermath of a deed. It's only tragic when the deed wasn't yours but you must live with the consequences, like a divorce, like a war, like an accident. It was not good enough to simply name a monster a monster like we do in books because a name is only a potential and does not become a soul until it finds its gripping in the soil, like a weed that does not know it is a weed until someone comes to pull it.

If this was going to be our last high school show, at least it was for a good cause. At this point, most of our gigs are in small bars in Providence and Boston (we even opened for Kansas at the local Fall River Celebrates America festival), so playing the high school feels a bit quaint. Playing at the high school always reminds me of Jess, and it is still new and raw enough in my memory to cause me pain. And all of this is thanks to Jess's mother, a woman I will hate for the rest of my life. Hate is dangerous, I know, but there are times when it must be upheld. Sometimes forgiveness is wrong and anger is the only way. There are people whose anger is noisy but does not actually reach their hearts, like Manny, and there are those who are slow to anger, like Em. There are those who are quick to anger but lack the fortitude to stay angry, like Ash, and there are those who know how to hold a serious and mature grudge, like me. We are the distance runners of forgiveness, the cross-country team. Not even death gets you out of jail free. There is no eleventh-hour forgiveness. When I go, I better be weighed rightly on Anubis's scale or else death is a big fake like a song with a sax solo. I don't want to die to the strains of studio saxophone, which has no place in a grunge song, anyway. "How do you talk to an angel?" Please.

Jess's mother never approved of the band. She didn't like my shaved head and knock-off purple Docs, or Manny's nose ring and black lipstick. And she absolutely detested Em's homemade shirts, especially the one with the maniac M&M brandishing a scimitar that said, *Eat me* on it. Of course, our parents hate those things too. I have clothes hidden all over town because my mother will throw them away if she finds them in my closet. She complains about my hair every single morning. She never misses a day. Portuguese mothers are nothing if not relentless when you don't do what they want. Jess's mother, however, went much further, calling us "the element," which was some big talk for a woman who worked the perfume counter at the Macy's in the sad little mall a town over—a hangout for retired folks and junior high kids. It didn't even have a movie theater. What kind of mall doesn't have a movie theater? Macy's thought working retail made her better than my parents, who worked in the failing textile mills with the other Portuguese people. According to Macy's, we were going nowhere and this band was nothing but a waste of time. Her daughter was going to Harvard; she was going to make something of herself. We were losers, common weeds.

To make matters worse, Jess is in the audience tonight. She hasn't been to one of our shows since leaving the band a few months ago. It hurt me that she would not come see us play, but I get it. It would be hard for me too. Maybe watching us play without her felt like betrayal. Few of us want the things we care about to exist without us, the fiction of our absolute necessity paramount. Or, maybe, she was happy to be free of us, to be free of the band's expectations, to move on without having to cut us free herself.

Before I know it, our set is almost over. I've missed almost the entire concert. We decided to end the show on a cover of Tool's "Sober." We don't play covers often anymore, though, like most bands, that is how we got our start, but we figured this song would be a fun one to end on. It doesn't have any special significance; it's just a song we play well, kicks a lot of ass, and gives Ash the opportunity to flop about the stage like a fish out of water—another of his stock imitations—this one of Faith No More's Mike Patton.

"Thanks for coming out tonight and supporting a great cause. For our last song," says Ash swiping the hair out of his eyes in that predetermined way we'd seen him do so often when he was putting the moves on some little groupie, "I'd like you to help me out." As a rule, we hate it when Ash riffs. He always says some dumb shit. Why do lead singers think every word that comes out of their mouths is poetry? Louder is not better, you dinks. Louder isn't more profound. It's like the little kids I give music lessons to who when asked to increase pitch increase volume instead. It's the same kind of misunderstanding, but they at least have their age as an excuse. Ash is just a dickhead. His giant hair literally makes him look like a penis. He is just acting accordingly, I guess.

"As some of you may know, our very own Jessie is in the audience tonight." The audience goes wild, which is the worst possible thing to happen. Ash eats up this kind of thing, and it encourages his bad behavior. The story of Jess's forced departure was well known and even people who hate us think Macy's acted poorly. Em mouths, "What is he doing?" I roll my eyes so far into my head they almost don't come back.

"It wouldn't be right to end our last show at the high school without her, don't you think?" The audience yells back, "Yes!" in unison. "What do you say, Jessie? Will you play with me one more time?" he says and raises his eyebrows, making a tacky reference to their former romantic relationship. No one is surprised by this behavior either. This is the same guy who grabbed his singing partner's ass while doing a cheesy duet from *Miss Saigon* in front of an audience of old ladies at the Venus de Milo banquet hall. The old ladies couldn't see what he was doing, but everyone in the chorus standing behind him could. It was a move totally calculated to increase his legend. It was so obvious, so insincere, and yet it totally worked. The man knew his business. He gave them what they wanted. Too bad it wasn't authentic in the least. I've known Ash almost as long as I've known Em and Manny, though we aren't really friends. Ash's birth name is Adam, no relation to the garden guy. In junior high school, he would spend homeroom drawing WWII war scenes with some creepy kid who basically wore Gestapo attire. How that Gestapo kid didn't get his ass kicked every day is a clear sign of our embarrassing ignorance of world events. In high school, however, when Ash found his voice, everything changed. A few bars of some cheesy love song and the right kind of girl would do whatever he wanted, and he knew it.

"Will you play with *us* one last time?" he amends and pauses letting the moment ferment. The look on Jess's face shows panic and a readiness to make a run for it. The fear I see can be best described as evolutionary, ancient, overmastering. Jess had gone toe-to-toe with her mother about the band a number of times and had lost. Jess is brave, but she knew she'd never be able to go to college without them. Harvard isn't their dream, it's hers. Just because it fit in with their little fantasy doesn't make it less real for Jess. She has a very pragmatic side. Jess loves music, is very talented, but she never wanted to be a professional musician. We knew this. We knew that even if the band got signed to a major label that it would probably be without her. That's what made what her mother did so unfair, and no amount of reason could move her mother's will. She would not see reason. She would not be moved.

But Ash is not going to let it go. The audience begins clapping and stomping their feet, chanting her name. Jess shakes her head no, stands and waves in a kind of thank you, hoping maybe that if she acknowledges the mob and then removes herself they might lose interest, but they will not let her leave. The cheering grows furious and I am starting to worry that something is about to go down. Now that high school is basically over, Ash doesn't care if they burn the place to the ground. There are always those in an audience waiting for a little chaos in order to create greater chaos, and Ash loves goading these people. Again, this is simply another imitation. In his mind, it is New Haven 1967 and there is a cop with a can of mace at the ready, and he, of course, is Jim Morrison. For the man who could sling the word "poseur" like a machete, he certainly had an interesting notion of his own authenticity. People near the stage start to shove against those pushing from the back of the room. A couple of trench-coated goons have chairs above their heads as if they are going to throw them, and I don't know what stops them. For some reason, a group to the left of the stage is bellowing war cries and throwing themselves bodily into the wall of the cafeteria. They don't seem to have the proper concept for slam dancing, or maybe they do. Whatever the switch for violence is, it has not been tripped yet, but I don't like this. Things are starting to get out of hand, and the audience will not let Jess escape, so she does the unthinkable and gives in. When she steps on stage, she hugs everyone except Ash. She fakes a hug and then jabs him in the cock with her open palm. Ash crumples to the ground in earnest and the comedy seems to ease the tension in the audience a little. Jess's hands are shaking so badly I am not sure she will be able to play, though I highly doubt anyone would notice considering the well-established crappiness of the drumming tonight. The other drummer hands over his sticks and slinks off stage, realizing that his lack of talent will be revealed; he will be revealed, or maybe that is just my fantasy. For all I know, he is proud of his performance. Of all the ideas I hate, I hate this one most of all.

Before Ash has the chance to start winding up the audience again, Em starts throbbing the bass line and taking the cue I kneel close into my amp to create ambient feedback. The audience becomes a mass of throbbing heads, whose rhythm soothes the chaos of a few moments ago. Manny takes the time to light a cigarette. He doesn't even smoke; he just likes lighting cigarettes on stage and letting them dangle from his lip, like Slash, like so many of our squinting uncles do when they play foosball, their obsession with soccer utter and complete. When the drums roll in, on time, I hit the opening lick hard and for the first time all night I feel it, feel in it, forget drummers and perfume counters and what awaits at summer's end. The music is whole, together, reaching out like a hand and grabbing the audience by the guts. A mosh pit breaks out and Ash—eyes closed—is giving

Maynard's lyrics the gravity they deserve, raking the meaning of those words one bit of skin at a time. He really can sing—lucky for him. When we get to the chorus, the band cuts out and everyone sings in unison, "Why can't we not be sober? I just want to start this over. Why can't we drink forever? I just want to start this over." We hadn't planned it. It just happened, one of those rare things. When the band kicks back in, I let Manny take the guitar line and jump into the audience, instrument and all, and someone gets a snapshot of The Great Gilgamesh riding a tidal wave of flannel shirts. Whoever took that picture gave me a great gift. I just didn't know it at the time. One last glorious picture of As Malcriadas as they were meant to be, for one moment all the pieces working together as they should.

Finally, here is something real, something only itself with no desires beyond voice and guitar, drums and bass, sweat and the swift feeling that the world could come crashing down and no one would notice, and that is the closest thing to being happy I have been in some time. I am riding on the hands of people I will likely never see again, though we have spent the majority of our short lives within spitting distance of one another. I'm going to ride this wave into the future and never look back. But the song is over far too quickly and though the sky holds its place, it might have been better had it crashed upon our heads and ground us to dirt. I know, even in the long present of that wonderful moment, that we'd lose Jess forever. And we did. When Macy's found out about the concert, she went completely mad. Ash is so fucking clueless, but we never would have had the chance to play that one last song together otherwise. I hate the way the world works against its own best interests so much of the time and how none of us were justly punished—only Jess, trapped in a monster's web.

EM
DASH

4

Though they often speak out of the sides of their mouths regarding most things American, our parents learned very quickly how to copy their holiday rituals: stockings hung from phony fireplaces, presents piled under plastic trees, and "Feliz Navidad" blaring on repeat from transistor radios hidden on kitchen counters among knick-knacks depicting the Azorean flag or the Cock of Barcelos—the magic rooster that saved an innocent Galician pilgrim from execution. Every year, Mr. Santos builds a monumental creche that takes up most of the living room. It includes a host of angels, townsfolk, donkeys, sheep, horses, the baby Jesus, of course, and—best of all—the three wise men travelling in caravan on model train tracks. It is impressive, to say the least. The only part of Portagee Christmas you won't find in the homes of our American friends is the long table in the parlor (a room we were never allowed in and where our parents kept their nice furniture, the statuary, the gilt mirrors, and the china), which was perpetually set with a sumptuous feast for holiday visitors, a feast worthy of an old folk tale. And like in those dark stories, woe to the child who so much as touches a cookie or a piece of cake for they will awaken a creature more horrifying than anything out of European folklore. These visitors can show up at any time of day or night for the duration of the holidays. They can—and often do—awaken the household at 3 AM and are welcomed with food and warm drinks boosted with shots of honey brandy, but I can't have even a single piece of candy, or the tiniest nibble of sweet bread or the littlest kiss of meringue. Somehow our mothers always knew. No amount of guile could fool them. No fleetness of foot could elude them. No stealth could blind them. No bonds could bind them. It was old magic.

"Your parents are ok with you having Christmas dinner with us?" asks Manny's mother for the tenth time today.

"Yup, they don't care."

"Ma," Manny says, in a South-Eastern Massachusetts way I was only now starting to notice. "Do we have to do this every single time?"

"They don't even know I'm home from school. It's all good."

"Emily, you should at least call them," Mrs. Santos says with a concerned eye that could kill when she wanted it to but which here rather held my heart in its hand.

"It's cool; we have an understanding."

"Let it go, Ma," Manny says, the word "Ma" becoming increasingly shrill each time he uses it.

"Wait till you have kids. You'll see."

Mrs. Santos is simply going through her usual routine. I've spent nearly every Christmas, Easter, and Thanksgiving over at Manny's since I was a kid. It was Mrs. Santos's way of protecting herself against the future, just in case she ever finds herself in the same position with her own son.

"Are you sure it's ok if I spend all break here?"

"You know you are always welcome in our house," says Mrs. Santos.

"But it's a whole month."

She raises her hand and chin in a way that will brook no more nonsense from me.

"João! Dinner." Even after all these years, I marvel at how loud Mrs. Santos can yell. It is a genuine gift. She is all of 4′11″ with heels on, but she screams up a few sizes, like those chimps who puff themselves up in order to intimidate rivals. She is a nice person but not to be trifled with. Everyone seems to simply understand this fact. It is a quality I wish to emulate—to be understood once and completely.

"Espera, mulher! The game is giving," responds Mr. Santos in that idiom particular to Fall River and its environs. For our parents, shows were "giving" rather than "on," like our American peers said. It was a literal translation of the verb "dar" or "to give" as in "*Dallas* está dando." Similarly, they "closed" the light in a room rather than shut it off, literally translating the verb "fechar," as in "Feche a luz."

"It's time to eat," she repeats in English so he'll get the point. Our mothers often used Portuguese in the same way American moms on television used middle names, to show they meant business, but they would reverse this with their husbands, using English when they weren't going to repeat themselves even one more time.

"OK. Wait a second," he hits back in kind.

This too is part of the domestic routine of the Santos household. When Mr. Santos isn't working, he is in the other room listening to his soccer game on the transistor radio, tinfoil on the bunny-ear antennae for better reception like every other Portuguese dad in the neighborhood. Considering how long I've known Manny, I don't really know very much about Mr. Santos. Like most of the fathers around here, he isn't there to be known. He goes to work and when he isn't at work, he is worrying about work. Or he mows his lawn. They have a sickness for lawns in this town, an obsession they share with their American neighbors. Everyone worries that aliens or robots will come to enslave us, but we have already been conquered by a simple weed. We do its bidding. Care for it. Nurture it; use up our own precious resources and time and strength to make it grow strong. Whoever heard of a weed that couldn't care for itself? Most weeds are impossibly hardy by definition. No matter the countermeasures, they grow. They find the smallest crack, drink the slightest water, find the least drop of sunlight in the deepest dark, survive months of scorching heat and long winters of deathly cold. They live. More than anything, they live.

When the game hits a lull, Mr. Santos comes to the table, and we can finally eat. There is no prayer, no giving of thanks for what one has earned with his own two hands, his sweat and blood, nothing like the kind of thing I have had to endure once or twice in Protestant homes. The Azoreans are Roman Catholics. They aren't like that kind of evangelical who can't believe in god without making a fuss, who can't feel faith unless everyone else does too—a collective fear of what the silence might bring. Immigrants go to church and keep their lips tight, except maybe once a year in confession at midnight Christmas mass. It is sometimes hard to tell a believer from the person simply doing what they think is expected of them from the community. This is what happens when entire villages emigrate at the same time. New country, same people, same expectations, same old rituals even when the rules are completely different. Manny only attended church as long as he did because it was the one time his parents weren't on top of him about going to work—and he got to hang out and pass notes with Gilga and me, though we already did this all week in school. Manny, like most people we knew, has worked since he was 14, jobs where the good people of our idyllic little New England town took every joy in treating us like dirt. Their smug faces when we pumped their gas, poured their coffees, cleaned their grubby plates, delivered their pizzas. Small towns are in every way small and they don't like it when you get too big for your britches.

The Santoses are good people (good enough, anyway). If there is something I am thankful for in this world, it is Manny's parents and their ancient hospitality—a hospitality old and iron-clad, unassailable, and unblinking even in the face of scarcity, especially in the face of scarcity. There would be nothing for me at my house. I'm not even sure my parents are home. They were known to leave town, as they did so often in my childhood, without even telling me, without leaving money for food, or concerning themselves about my safety. They were not like other Portuguese parents. They were Boomers. The immigrants were not Boomers. They did not grow up in the lazy privilege of that giant generation. The immigrants were adults. Our parents didn't know how to have fun, or rather they feared someone was going to send them a bill. Everything had a price tag. They had issues, to be sure, but they were grown-ups, at least. They were the same age as the Boomers but they couldn't be more different. I felt the distance in my bones. My parents knew nothing beyond their petulance. Where had they learned such behaviors? My grandparents were so frugal and self-effacing they'd give you the clothes on their backs without needing to be asked. It's no surprise they never got along with their children, and why my parents don't get along with me.

The Santoses, however, are way in over their heads when it comes to Manny. There are only Portuguese in our families going back hundreds of years, maybe longer, but something tells me Manny isn't going to continue the line in a way they will find acceptable. He dates infrequently, so his parents have been spared the grief for the moment, but it will come crashing down soon enough, I am sure. When someone without a Portuguese last name calls the house, Mrs. Santos pretends not to speak English and hangs up on him, though this is a common-enough tactic with all the Portuguese mothers. I think his parents like keeping me around because they hope we'll end up together, but they are barking up the wrong tree on this one. Manny and I don't swing that way; we're more like siblings. I think they are hoping we'll fall in love because Manny also likes boys. I suspect they know this, but they would never say anything about it out loud. The Portuguese have a great capacity for silence. If you don't name a thing, it doesn't exist, or so they are hoping.

"What are you two doing today?" asks Mrs. Santos.

"We have band rehearsal."

"On Christmas Eve?"

"We're going into the studio next week to record our album and we haven't played together in months."

"Mrs. Mello doesn't want you making all that noise in her house on Christmas."

"They're not home. They're doing visitas all day. We asked." During the Christmas holidays, our families would visit everyone they knew. They called it visitas. It was the one time where the parlors—sealed off against any childish incursion during the rest of the year—were decked out with all kinds of cakes, nuts, cookies, figs, and candies. It was a week-long feast where the only point was to show your hospitality, to host and be hosted, to show plenty before returning to the austerity of their day-to-day.

Mr. Santos slams the table with his fist and all the plates rattle. "Jesus, João!"

"Desculpe, sorry, sorry, Maria. It's 1-1." Mr. Santos leaves the room with a beer to finish listening to his beloved soccer team, Benfica. Everything is going according to script.

"João, feche a luz. You're wasting electricidade."

"I just sat down. Manny, close the light for Daddy, ok?"

Manny's parents are the closest thing to normal I have. Manny would lose his mind at the idea that he is some kind of model of normal for me. If anyone is *The Wonder Years* around here, it is him, or as close to it as we get. All you need to do is exchange the 60s soundtrack for fado and football for soccer and you've got it. Manny doesn't know what it is like to have parents who don't know what college you go to. I would even take Jessie's mother. She may be batshit crazy and racist as hell, but she, at least, knows when her daughter's birthday is. My parents wouldn't be able to pick me out of a lineup. Though it was Manny who fell beneath the ice the winter he turned 8, I know what it is like beneath the dark water too. It is a place you can't talk your way out of, a place you can't wish away or bargain with. And if you do make it back somehow, like Manny did, you don't always come back whole.

GOMEZ ADDAMS

5

AMHERST 1996

I met Manny in the dorm, in the bathroom actually. I was drying off after a shower when the person in the next stall pulled back his shower curtain. I don't think I did a very good job hiding my surprise. He, on the other hand, played it cool, like he did this all the time. We lived on a floor reserved for freshman, so it is not very likely he had any more experience with public showers than I did, but he certainly played it off better than me. Maybe he had been an athlete and was used to showering with other men. The showers at my high school were never used. Boys would rather smell like balls and gym shoes than get naked in front of one another. Small towns—as if anyone gave a shit about seeing them naked. I met him again a few weeks later at a party in the RA's room and we discovered our mutual love for New Wave. When he asked me my name, I told him it was Gomez, Gomez Addams.

"Like from *The Addams Family*?" he asked, raising an eyebrow.

"Exactly," I said, "from the movie, not the TV show." He nodded in perfect comprehension. But it was he who was dashing, not me, with those same bright eyes and dark features of Raul Julia. I walked him to his room later, and he invited me to stop by anytime I would like. I wanted to stop

33

by at that moment, but I was afraid, and I ran for it, but not without promising I would return someday. When I leave for class in the mornings, I pass the window to his room, and I pass it again late at night, returning from my favorite Amherst café. His light is almost always on, and often I hope to catch a glimpse of his shadow as he passes.

Tonight, as I am returning from a long session in the library, I see the light on as usual, "Pictures of You" blaring from the open window, and something moves me to risk calling up to him. It's late. Everything is covered in a foot of snow and nuzzled in its distinct kind of silence and this gives me courage. From this distance, I am brave. I call out, doing a poor imitation of a blackbird. He hears after my second attempt and comes to the window, adjusting a bathrobe hastily over his shoulders. Everyone knows when you knock on a dorm door, you have to wait longer than normal to give the person time to put some pants on. Like everyone else, I spend most of my time when my roommate is away totally naked. "Cyrano," Manny says, "is that you?"

"Excuse me?"

"That makes me sad. You really didn't plan this very well, did you?" Manny jokes.

"No, I guess not."

"Cyrano always comes bearing poetry and a pretty face to say the words."

"Strikeout on both counts, I'm sorry to say."

"I'm not so sure about that. Come on up," he says, and waves me up to his room.

It occurs to me that I have never done this before. My whole life, I have only ever dated women. I like women, but I have also always known that I like boys too, but there was no place for that kind of thing in my high school. And just because I know something about myself, doesn't mean I know how to do it in real life. If I screw this up, not only will I be stuck living next to this guy for the rest of the year, but it might do all kinds of long-term damage to the idea of who I think I am or want to be. The risk is real, but I don't want to be beholden to an idea any longer. I will gladly carry the weight of a truth, even if it means untold amounts of humiliation—or so I tell myself.

As I approach the door, I hear Manny tuning his guitar. Manny, as Gilga would say, is the Boy Who Plays Guitar in Stairwells. Every college has them. They are almost a cliché, if they weren't so damn cute. The acoustics in stairwells are surprisingly excellent if you like a lot of reverb, and he's not old enough yet to feel bad about serenading an entire dorm population. Of course, with everyone's stereos blaring Pink Floyd day and night (whether they are in their rooms or not— mostly not) most people probably can't hear him, anyway.

He lets me in when I knock, still wearing only a robe, which is a relief and a dread. He invites me to sit on his bed next to him because there isn't anywhere else to sit. Each dorm room has one chair and two beds, which means the chairs are often repurposed as shelf space or as dirty laundry hampers. And you don't want to sit on the roommate's bed. Who knows what atrocities have been committed there, so, you see, we were out of options.

"Play for me," I say, as if I had just thought of it and not planned it as I was waiting outside his door. He walks around the room lighting candles before picking up his guitar again. It seems rehearsed and yet innocent.

"This is just a first draft, ok? I haven't worked out all the lyrics, and I'm not much of a singer," he says a little defensively. His little caveat helps me feel less tense because I am having the hardest time trying to read him. I'm a little glad to find he cares about my opinion. I try to get comfortable on his bed, dismissing his excuses with a wave of the hand, trying desperately to hide the fact that I am panic sweating. I am desperately trying to impress him with my coolness, and I am likely not pulling it off. I have a terrible poker face. He tells me it is a new song he is working on for his band. He had told me at the party that his band was going into the studio over winter break and were still short a couple of songs to make a full album, which I think is totally awesome. Why has everyone else done so much more than me? What the hell is driving these people? At 18, they have done more than some people do their entire lives. I haven't done a damn thing worth mentioning. As he plays, time stretches and bends and slows to his strumming cadence: the candles flicker, the wind blows down the spine of the orchard hill outside the window, the wood of the bed creaks like pain and cracking knuckles when I move. Moments like these are so rare and fragile that every time I hear some undergrad stomping down the hall, rattling all the doors as they pass, I fear the spell will be broken. Thankfully, the snow continues to glow at the edge of what is otherwise a very large and still busy campus even at this hour and protects the moment from intrusion. Something like a baby's cry thrums in the white noise between his breaths. Something like ice rises in the layers of the chords, something deep at the bottom of a frozen pond.

Manny has his eyes closed and is visibly sweating. UMass keeps the dorms unusually hot so we often have to keep the windows open, and Western Mass gets freezing cold during the winter months. My roommate is from Hong Kong and he had never seen snow before. As we were leaving for class after the first snow of the season, I started to say, "Be careful of the …" and before I could get the word "ice" out, he was on his butt. But the dorm is a sweat box, though I don't think that is why Manny is sweating. He is not here at the moment, not really, one of those special things performers can do the rest of us cannot. Manny is swaying, volucrine in his commitment to his words, which sound comfortable in his mouth, his top lip twisting every now and then in a way I find very appealing—a snaggle tooth in his lower jaw jutting out like volcanic rock in the ocean surrounding my parents' village in the Azores. He opens his eyes and meets mine, as if he knows I am looking. Everything goes quiet like when you duck your head beneath the bath water, one of those special moments when the restless noises of college students abate, and I hear what sounds like whistling, like a blackbird sitting on a roof, the call I was trying to imitate at his window.

My heart is pounding so loud I fear the world itself might crack beneath its concussion. And then, it happens. The one thing that should never happen. The one thing I will never live down; the turning point that would define my romantic life as a failure until I died. I simultaneously look surprised and try to pretend I didn't hear it. Manny looks at me and cocks his head like a puppy, a small smile on his face. This cannot be happening. It did not happen. I am not here, and then I die. Ok, I don't die; I just wish to die. My stomach has always been my enemy. When I am nervous, it begins gurgling and spinning it can be heard across the room. It is so loud sometimes that people will ask me to repeat what I just said because they've confused the ghastly noises my intestines are making for human speech. "Please," I think to myself, "please, let it be a dream."

"Did you just toot?" says Manny in a way that is so cute I almost forget the horror of the moment.

"Sorry," I manage to sputter in-between bouts of hemming and hawing. "My stomach has always been a mess," I say, unable to look into his deep, clay-brown eyes. The world returns to its old flabby shape in an instant.

"Feel better?" he asks, and I give him a desperate look. He replies, "You looked a little tense. Don't worry. It's exactly what we needed to lighten the mood." Damn, my poker face has failed me again. He could tell how nervous I was long before I destroyed every last scrap of magic in the world. Why couldn't I be cool, just once? Being cool has got to do with courage, with risk on the brink of disaster, of being able to carry it off even if you mess up. I have never been confident enough to be reckless.

"What do we do now?" I say, clearing my throat, trying to get beyond this moment, looking at the door as if I might actually make a break for it.

"I know, let's play Truth or Dare," says Manny, as if he has been waiting for the right time to make this suggestion since I walked in the door. "Or, maybe a little Spin the Bottle?" he says and spins an imaginary bottle which points directly at me. "You know you want to." I do want to. More than anything.

"Do I?" I manage to say, throat parched and tight.

"Uh huh," he nods confidently. "I'm onto you."

"Is that right?"

"Yep," he says popping the "p" comically.

"Whatever do you mean?" I drawl in a terrible Blanche Dubois accent. He gives me that same little head tilt, but this time the smile is replaced by an upturning of lips which indicates confusion. Manny decides to take the initiative and put me out of my misery by dramatically dropping his robe, daring me, trying to get me to give in to the spirit of the game. He is wearing nothing but boxer shorts. His thin body is lined with long, lean muscle and his chest bears a tattoo of gears slowly transforming into crows that connects shoulder to shoulder all in black, which is so sexy. Images of time and transformation, he'll tell me later, and I'll trace the curves of the gears as they fly into pieces and become Odin's crows.

A magic door reveals itself only when the proper conditions have been met, which is what differentiates a magic door from an ordinary one, and I think I knew it before we even sat down, knew the possibility of it, the certainty of it, the moment I entered his room. The table is set, but one must never partake of the feast in the monster's house; everyone knows that, but everyone does it, anyway. One taste and the monster awakens; one taste and the door shuts forever. I think of Manny's young face and easy laugh. I think of his smooth silhouette drifting like a sweeping of stairs at the edge of porch light, his shadow looming languidly around corners.

"Well?" he says, though I don't see his lips move. "It's just magic, baby," say his crows circling the room now, turning like gears, swooping like portents.

"Well, if it's only magic," I say and drop my pants to my ankles and chase him around the room. He feigns fear and runs away, comically slow—my role, the monster; his role, the wolf in disguise fanging like Red Riding Hood. When Manny lets me catch him, we are still laughing and breathing hard from our parody of chase, and he leans in for a kiss, which is what I have been wanting to do from the moment I saw him in the shower. He is right. Being silly makes me brave; it makes me reckless, and though it isn't the same thing as cool, it still gets me where I need to go. I sense something edging the room and see its shadow sheer and slip off my shoulders like a silk kimono, my arms spreading wings to meet his forelegs and wolf paws. What are these weeds, these roots? What claws? What wings? Then the candles blow out.

THE GREAT GILGAMESH

6

PROVIDENCE 2015

When we met, I told Ian my name was The Great Gilgamesh and he looked at me like I was crazy.

"What's your real name?"

"That is my real name."

"The one your parents gave you."

"Oh, I don't know. I forget."

"You're weird."

"Ok, nice meeting you, whoever you are," I said and began stomping across the room as quickly as I could.

"I'm Ian."

"Good for you, Ian," I tossed over my shoulder.

"Where are you going?"

I was already half way across the room before I heard something earnest in the way he asked the question. Normally, I would have just kept going because one of the joys of being an adult is not having to spend unnecessary amounts of time with assholes, but it quickly became clear to me he wasn't trying to be one; he was just utterly, totally, profoundly, confoundingly clueless. Why am I always attracted to people like this, to the One Who Doesn't Know, as my friends used to say, because he was clearly it! Many people hide malice beneath

41

earnestness, but for the Ones Who Don't Know malice is usually the farthest thing from their minds. Was their earnestness a recompense for a lifetime of awkward interactions with other humans? It is only natural to love in others one's deepest faults, or so I try to convince myself.

When I was little, there was a neighborhood girl I'd see around a lot. We weren't friends, just members of a large loosely-affiliated crew of kids who lived on the block. We both lived on the "right" side of the tracks but didn't belong there at all, our parents reaching beyond their means towards a dream that would always elude them, like we would always elude them. We weren't fooling anyone with our off-brand clothes and bad teeth, but that's what I liked about her. One day, and for reasons I barely understood at the time and have wasted much time since trying to remember, we got into a fight and she raked her fingernails across my left cheek, then slashed me with the right before I could so much as blink, drawing blood and leaving scars that appear when exhaustion ghosts my skin back from my face. And even though I wrenched loose a chunk of her hair in retaliation, she made me cry because I knew she liked me and I liked her more than friends, but, somehow, I screwed it all up and it ended in blows. And I cried because I was not cool and would never be and now everyone knew it. I cried because I was the Girl Who Didn't Know.

Ian has the annoying habit of insisting on my "real" name, which I refuse to answer to: sometimes on purpose, other times because I honestly don't realize he's talking to me. I think our relationship is founded on this basic disagreement. My whole life my friends called me The Great Gilgamesh—a name I inherited more than a name I was given, a name to live up to or drown under. But that's who I am, The Great

Gilgamesh—no relation to the Sumerian king and his great walled Uruk. My so-called real name never really made any sense. It was a label, more like a brand than a true name. Ian always says, "I can't introduce you as The Great Gilgamesh to my colleagues." Like we ever go anywhere with his colleagues. What colleagues? Most nights, he comes home for dinner and then goes straight to bed. And he can sleep through anything like the Sumerian king caught in a sad and obvious lie of sleep. If the house caught fire, there would be no rousing him, and I am not going to try and carry him, that's for sure. I am responsible for getting our daughter out of the house and that's as much as I can do in an emergency. Once I gave birth to Lilly, Ian became responsible for his own escape plan. I'm not saying I wouldn't make every attempt to get him out of the house, but when I say he won't wake up, I'm not exaggerating. I told him we should build a ramp or a slide that goes from the bed to the window so that I can just shove him down it. The bedroom is on the ground floor. He'd probably be fine, but he just gives me the same "you're weird" look and walks away.

When Lilly was a baby, I did all the night work and not just because I was breastfeeding. And even now, when Lilly wets the bed or has a nightmare, I'm the one who changes the sheets or listens to the telling of the scary dreams, especially the one about the telephone. Only my child would have nightmares about phones. I hate them too. Can such a thing be passed in the genes, the momentary panic of an AMBER alert, the storm warning, the twister on its way in the pea-green sky. It's the result of growing up with parents who don't speak English and who make you the liaison to this alien world, as if a child has any business dealing with the bank or the doctor or the insurance company. And things have not improved in my adulthood. I never answer the damn thing if I can help it. I put off official phone calls as long as possible. I never complain when the delivery guy messes up my order. Ian just looks at me like I've lost my mind. He does not understand the panic of being responsible before you are ready. Whenever the phone rings, I know something bad has happened. It's usually the school calling because Lilly threw a Lego block across the room, or she smashed another kid's card house, or she punched someone in the eye, though the other kid probably started it. Last week I arrived at school to find Lilly squirming in the teacher's arms as if she was on fire—and since it was the end of the day, all the parents stared at me like this was some kind of novel parenting technique. Like any good parent, I am not fair when it comes to my daughter. I cannot be reasoned with. I cannot be bargained with, like a hurricane, like a tidal wave, like a season. I am not cool and I do not care.

When Lilly was born, she didn't cry. She opened her blackbird's eyes, looked around the room for a couple of seconds as if weighing the value of the world of light and then shut them. The world had been judged and I can't say I disagreed with her. She is already more like me than anyone else on this dirt ball and I knew it. I knew it like something impossible and yet on its way. And she didn't open her eyes again for a month, and I couldn't blame her. The very first night in the hospital, though I was at my limits from the fourteen-hour labor, I woke at 3 AM to the sound of Lilly's little cheeps, her bird's version of crying. She had somehow managed to slip out of her wrap and Ian, who was sleeping in the chair right next to her, didn't hear a thing. I wobbled out to find a nurse because I didn't know how long she had been in the open air, and it was freezing in that room. Why are hospitals like meat lockers? I know the cold is to stop the spread of viruses so deadly their names could be taken from the roster of void monsters older than the oldest gods, but the poor thing could've died of exposure right there in the room with her parents asleep a few feet away and no shepherd in sight to lumber her to a nearby kingdom. When the nurses checked her, it turned out she was in fact having some issues maintaining her body temperature, so I had to stay in the hospital a few extra days until she stabilized, which was fine with me. It was better than going home. I was too scared to be alone with a baby, though I already loved her more than anyone that ever was.

It's not really Ian's fault if I'm being fair. He works hard and he's good at what he does, I guess. He's an intellectual property lawyer, but he does not work for a firm. He is freelance so the work comes all at once or not at all. And the money's not as good as you think when you factor in that we are not insured nor does he have a retirement plan through an employer. The hours are terrible. Even when he's home, he's not home. The phone rings every ten minutes—always some new issue that can't be resolved without him. The only uninterrupted time he has is when he's in bed, and it's like his body will not allow anything to break up the rare monotony of sleep. He works hard, but I work hard too. I'm on the clock full time and then I can't sleep in the new house we just bought. It has been a long time since any of us have lived in an actual house. It is small—a little raised ranch in Providence, RI—but it has large windows on both the west facing and east facing sides of the house, which gives us stunning sunrises and sunsets and makes the gold color we chose for the living room glow. No more institutional white for me. That was the one rule I had. I didn't care what kind of house we bought or where we bought it so long as we immediately repainted any and all white walls.

The moon makes its way across the sky. I can watch it climb up my living room window and then watch it soft back down toward the horizon from my dining room. Lilly turns in her bed and I hold my breath. Her medications make her a little bit of a zombie and sometimes she gets up to pee and gets confused. When we first moved into the house, she walked into the kitchen, sat down at the table and peed, and then went back to bed like nothing happened. She thought she was in the bathroom at the old apartment. Her inner compass was working a little too well. I couldn't do anything but laugh about it as I mopped pee off the black and white tiles of my new kitchen. Kids.

Ian doesn't want to be responsible for anything having to do with Lilly, so he forces me to make all decisions. He just keeps saying he doesn't know—the Boy Who Doesn't Know. How does he fall? Is it, like this? Like a plate? Or is it like this? Like a Sumerian's wild grief at the death of his companion?

EM DASH

7

We return late from rehearsal. The band didn't sound good—
at all. It was easy to see into Gilga's mind. She realized all
at once that none of us had been practicing, that while we
claimed to be excited about the idea of going into the studio,
none of us had actually done the work. Ash kept forgetting
lyrics, and I was pretty lousy too. I'm no Kim Gordon to begin
with but tonight I was all thumbs in the conventional sense—
not in that funky slap-bass way. I had intended to practice,
had, in fact, picked up my bass a bunch of times but just had
too much to do. Even Manny was unsure in his playing, and
he's usually one of the steadier musicians, taking his job as
rhythm guitarist very seriously. Manny paid great attention to
the slight differences in the musical structure that made one
song compelling and another ordinary. He understood how
a little guitar lick could sparkle, how the right chord could fill
out a conventional blues structure so it sounded like something new, and he didn't need you to know, which is why it
worked so well. They were his songs, after all. Well, half his,
anyway. On the bright side, it seems Gilga has finally managed
to find a drummer worth his salt. He's a young kid, still in high
school, and he kind of grew up on our band. He regaled us

with stories of riding his BMX by Jess's house to listen to us practice our versions of "Even Flow" or "Rooster," so much flannel even in the deep humidity of New England summer.

We were so grunge in those days we literally started out in a garage. The new kid can actually play, and at this point he knows the songs better than we do. I gave him the name Kid because he looked just like Prince in *Purple Rain*. Kid is Portuguese Prince, even dresses like him, which makes him kind of stick out in our flannel outfit, but we are nothing if not eclectic. Ash welcomed Kid into the mysteries of the band by telling him the sordid tale of how he might or might not have slept with Kid's sister the night before his Holy Confirmation. Our church made us all go on a weekend retreat before we could be Confirmed and thus become full members of the congregation. For most of us, it is the last time we ever step foot in a church short a wedding or baptism. Well, Ash manages to sneak out Saturday night. He had planned it far in advance, counting on the fact that adult supervision would likely be skimpy. He was correct. Some friends picked him up and he spent his last night of spiritual reflection before Confirmation day getting totally and completely wasted on 40s and Goldschläger. The next morning, he woke up next to Kid's sister, hungover and still rather high. He had the wherewithal to sneak back into the church basement without being seen by the adults mere minutes before High Mass. Though the adults were generally clueless, his escapade had not gone unnoticed by his peers, who got one smell of him and knew exactly what he'd been up to, and he was fooling no one in church, listing to one side or other as his equilibrium punished his late-night transgressions. Ash likes to refer to it as his Excommunication. It's why we started calling him Ash Wednesday.

Most of us get saddled with a nickname that is not one we would choose for ourselves. Ash, on the other hand, loved every ironic bit of this name. He never could stop himself from wagging his little dick around, couldn't relax until Kid knew his place in the band hierarchy. But if he was trying to get a rise out of Kid, he failed miserably. Kid, in his purple crushed velvet suit and pirate shirt, his eyes lined in dark eye liner, was far too cool for such a base move. He seemed to understand that Ash was nothing more than a collective hallucination, a contract that could not last long under close scrutiny. He was a name in lights. Kid couldn't take personally what obviously had nothing to do with him or his sister, for that matter. I would have punched him in the throat, hurt him where it counts, but that's just me.

Manny is taking a shower and Mr. and Mrs. Santos are either in bed or are out doing their visitas. I didn't want to disturb them just in case, so I kept the volume on the TV down. Rehearsal was long and stressful and the water rushing in the pipes is making me sleepy in a way I haven't been in months. The dorms rarely get quiet during the best of times and on weekends it's absolute pandemonium—warring stereos endlessly playing *The Dark Side of the Moon* for some inexplicable reason, glass breaking at irregular intervals, and the sad sounds of near-perpetual vomiting. College kids are totally gross. It feels good to be home, but I can't stay too long. The longer I stay, the harder it is to convince myself that the past four months have been real. How easy it is to fall back into old rhythms. My first college semester had, barely a week ago, felt like relief so deep it touched the roots that had made their way beneath the rocks and into the soil that smells like life and death, like I had finally started real life, like I had escaped some terrible dream; but back in Somerset, I lose that certainty and am no longer sure I will ever return to a world more marvelous than any entered through a wardrobe.

Dinner with the Santoses earlier today felt so right; spending time with the band—lousy rehearsal and all—felt right too, was like remembering a song you once loved before you had a clear picture of what you were and what you could never be. It was only now that I understood that at school I am a planetary body falling through space, never really resting, hurtling at unthinkable speeds towards some indeterminate and distant spot. I yearned to get closer to that spot, but it frightened me as well. The distances were great, maybe too great for someone like me. What monsters? What marvelous beasts? What secrets hidden in the orbits of new stars?

"Man, we sucked tonight."

I open my eyes to find Manny in his bathrobe munching on some shortbread cookies—his perpetual sweet tooth at work.

"We sucked something awful," I agree.

"How did we get so bad so quickly?"

"Not looking too good, is it? Studio is what, next week?"

"We'll get it together."

"I thought Gilga was going to stab us all to death."

"She still might."

At rehearsal, Gilga had the look of someone planning damage, but who couldn't decide if it was worth it or not. In the end, she said nothing; she did nothing, but I know her well enough to know she was not happy and her disappointment could be nasty and lasting. Jess's mother, for example, would never see the resolution of Gilga's anger. The universe just wasn't going to be around long enough. I hated to disappoint her; the world was already so full of disappointment.

Maybe we honestly thought we could simply pick up where we left off, but, I knew now, without Gilga around, without the wood-paneled walls of the rehearsal space, the band faded into the fog where good intentions that never get acted on go. Without Gilga, we couldn't raid the fog and find a way out, so we did nothing but hang back at the edge of effort where it was safe.

Suddenly, I hear a faint sound coming from the direction of the picture window. It is faint enough I am not sure I hear it, like the sound glass makes when you heat and cool it too quickly, or the sound steel makes when you quench it in water and find a crack. A few seconds later, another, something bouncing off the plate glass window, I realize.

"Did you hear that?" I say. We stop to listen. "There it is again. What the hell is it?" I go over to make sure the door is locked. Manny skulks up to the window and moves the curtains very slowly, trying to get a look at the front yard, not that he can see much in the dark. And then, a bad imitation of a bird call, the kind you make by cupping your hands and blowing between your thumbs. "Oh my god. You idiot," says Manny all of a sudden and runs past me to the door.

"What is it?"

Manny throws open the door and runs outside giggling in a way I have never seen in my whole life. Manny giggling. He runs into the front yard with his bathrobe coming undone and then something emerges from the bushes lining the driveway. He flings himself into the shadow's arms, laughing. "What are you doing here, you crazy person?" I hear him say from my spot in the doorway.

"Surprise!" a young man's voice says. And then they fall headlong into the bushes like a couple of drunk college kids laughing and kissing—the rest of the world forgotten in a way only the young can manage. I stand backlit in the doorway and in that moment something clicks in me in that calm way that feels like fear, in that way that changes things forever. I notice my shadow looks wrong, the silhouette not quite matching the shape I have come to know. What I do know, however, what I can't unknow—as Gilga would say—is that high school is finally, truly over. High school doesn't actually end with graduation, it ends soon after when the past becomes impossible to change, a finished act, all the coloring done and no more shapes to fill. How does it end? Like this? Like the answer to a simple question? Like a question answered with another question? Or is it, like this? An incomplete phrase, a fake bird call, a tumble into the bushes?

THE GREAT GILGAMESH

8

"Six years! Six years? Jesus, Gilga! What have you been doing with yourself?"

I shake my head instead of answering. Em always stops by when she's in town, and when Lilly was born five years ago, she came out for an entire month and slept on my couch just to help out. I hadn't spoken to her in years, not since we were kids, not since the band had broken up the summer of 1996. I had long hoped to reconcile with her, but I couldn't find her on social media and she didn't come to any of the high school reunions—not that this surprised me. Em had no school spirit and found most of these nostalgia-building events distasteful. Smells like teen spirit and all that. I had promised never to go myself, but I have gone to every single one. I can't help it. I don't feel the same antipathy towards my hometown I used to, though I'd never live there. For years, no one could find her. Manny took it the hardest. Even by our standards, they were close, the closest. Em had saved him, had found help when he had fallen beneath the ice. They were bound to one another from that point on, or so we all thought. A bond can become a boundary, a suture, a limit, it seems.

One night, however, just after Lilly was born, I got a call. I couldn't believe it was really her. She said she was in town for her grandmother's funeral and had heard about the baby, so she was hoping I'd let her visit. I absolutely wanted to see her. I was desperate for friends.

To be fair to my other friends, Manny and Gomez do pop in once in a while to see Lilly. I wish they didn't have to live so far away. Babies are tough to deal with but new parents are tougher still. It's so hard to make new friends when you have a baby. Sometimes people forget to adjust their parameters for young children. A baby, for example, has no way of earning her keep. She cannot dazzle with her conversation or wit, nor can she be held accountable for her actions. She does not pick you for your good qualities or shun you for your failures. She doesn't care who's naughty and who's nice. As for me, I cannot help it. Just the memory of the smell of her head makes me feral to protect her. Knowing this does nothing to combat the feeling. And that's what makes new parents notoriously tedious, and I know I left tedious about a mile back bleeding in the dust with hyenas circling. But I guess it's truly one of those things you can't understand until you're in the middle of it yourself. It used to piss Manny off really bad when parents said things like this— that you couldn't understand what they were going through until you went through it—because most of the time that is just some bullshit. I get what he means, but in this case, he happens to be wrong. The fate of those with strong opinions is to be wrong, especially at 40. Turning 40 is an exercise in how wrong one can be, but it is also a test. If you know love need not reduce you to cinders and still give you all you desire if not what you deserve, then you pass the test. I remember when 40 was an impossible number, some value that simply meant many, like in the Bible.

Em seemed to really love my little girl right from the first moments—a love like an accident, like falling down the stairs.

She seemed to understand her in some profound and basic way even I didn't, no matter how exhausting or single-minded it was being around Lilly. The doctors say Lilly has ASD and so most people don't understand her. It's mild enough that they mistake her extreme behaviors for bad temper or poor child rearing—depending on who they are in the mood to judge. But not Em. She knew who Lilly was before Lilly had words enough to tell her. Em is song. Em is a perfect lyric even when misheard or maybe especially when misheard. She's Jeff Buckley's "Love, let me sleep tonight on your couch." She's Tracy Chapman's "ticket to anywhere." She's Layne Staley's "Name your god and be afraid." She's the kind who shows up randomly with coffee, the kind who lets you cry exhausted tears without judgement. It is Em who bought Lilly the cat toys that saved my sanity. Lilly was so restless all the time but wouldn't play with any of the toys we got her, the ones all the other parents were just dying over. She showed zero interest in TV. I kept telling the damn doctors she was bored, but they patronizingly assured me that a child so young could not be bored. I tried everything: car rides, baby swings, rattles, hyp-notically weird kid's songs; nothing worked. Walks worked for a bit, but only when it was really cold out. Lilly liked the frost, was happiest with wind-burnt cheeks and her little tongue numb from the cold. She wouldn't open her eyes like when she was born, but her tongue was perpetually flicking out, tasting the temperature of cold, my sweet little serpent. One day Em shows up with some textured cat chew toys with bells in them and Lilly just loves them. It was the texture. Lilly didn't like the smooth texture of all those expensive toys. She wanted to bite into something her teeth could hold onto. She would play with those toys sometimes for ten minutes. Ten minutes! Ten whole minutes where I could just sit on the couch and catch a nap while Lilly squeaked in her mewling language. Sometimes I didn't even make it to the couch. I'd just fall over on the floor at baby height, dead to the world.

"Six years! Jesus, Gilga! What have you been doing with yourself?"

"You know what I've been doing with myself."

"But, six years. How do you live?"

"I don't know, Em. This is so hard."

"Why?"

"Why? I don't know why. Who knows why Ian does anything."

I haven't told anyone this before, even Em. It is too private. Plus, I was certain things would change, and I didn't want there to be weirdness between my friends and my partner. You know how that goes. You get into a fight and spend the night trashing your partner with your best friend but by morning your anger has cooled; however, now your friend knows more than they should. It's like the scene in *Mr. & Mrs. Smith* where Brad Pitt finds out his wife is a rival assassin and he, in a very endearing way, protects her from Vince Vaughn's verbal assault because Brad is certain they will get back together, that they will overcome this "small" complication. But after six years, I am getting desperate. Honestly, it would have been easier if Ian had been moonlighting as an assassin. That, at least, was something I could hold onto, something I could bite into.

"Do you ... have someone else?"

"Hell no. You know I don't do that shit."

"No judgment."

"No, I don't."

"Well ... why not?"

"Would you?"

"I don't know."

"See?"

"No, I wouldn't have someone on the side, but I also would not be with someone who refused to have sex with me for six years."

"Relationships are about more than just sex, though, right?"

"Of course, but that doesn't mean sex isn't important."

"I mean, I would be ok with no sex if he would snuggle me or kiss me. Hell, if he would just sit with me holding hands," I say.

"It seems to me the problem isn't really sex."

"What am I going to do?"

"Got me, menina. I haven't been in a serious relationship, well, ever, so I don't know what I'm talking about and shouldn't be giving anyone advice," says Em.

"I guess I don't either."

When Ian and I first met, I had just gotten out of a relationship with a semi long-term girlfriend. I'd had boyfriends before but for some reason none of them became serious. By that point, I had basically given up on men. I told everyone I was gay, which wasn't exactly true but not a lie either. It was too much work trying to explain so I just stopped explaining. Being bisexual sucks—if that's even the right word for what I am. Bisexual, bisexual plus, pansexual: I don't know. The fact is gender just doesn't play into my romantic desires. Too queer to be straight, too straight to be queer—the complexity lost in the oversimplifications of false binaries.

It's a cliché to say he was not like anyone I had ever dated before, but it does happen to be true, to some extent. I hate it when clichés come true because then you're stuck in the rut of it when retelling the story—even to yourself. I imagine the same thing is true about divorces, which have been on my mind a lot lately. One person, at least, gets forever trapped in the sad and usually boring narrative of the failed marriage, gets trapped reacting to someone else's decision. If Ian and I go down for the count, I am going to do something outrageous just so we have a good story to tell. I won't condemn him to having to tell the story of how I slept with my boss, which I don't have, or his best friend, which he doesn't have, or whatever boring crap usually kills marriages. I love him too much for that, I guess. To take someone's life story and shit all over it is unforgivable, almost worse than the betrayal itself. I'm going to do something mad—something so wild Ian's next partner will blanche and wonder what on earth he ever saw in me in the first place. Ian won't, so he's left me with little choice. Maybe I'll lose myself in the desert or book passage on a ship to the Arctic before it disappears. I'll marry Koko the Gorilla and we'll raise Lil together. Yes, Koko would understand. How do you sign, "I love you?"

Just before I met Ian, I had made the rule that I would not date any more Pisces, theater people, or musicians. For some reason I attract people who fit all three of these criteria. I was tired of their nonsense. I wanted something different.

"Have you talked to him about it?"

"Many times, querida."

"And nothing?"

"Yeah, for a day or two. But I'm still the one who does all the work. He kind of endures it; he doesn't seem to enjoy it at all. He won't initiate, just lies there and I'm supposed to be grateful because it's better than him not touching me at all. At this point, I just want to be seduced. Don't laugh. I swear, how did I end up a sex-starved, suburban housewife? It's ridiculous."

"Very Danielle Steel."

"She's Portuguese-American, you know," I say.

"No fucking way."

"Yes. Too bad she, like so many Portuguese-Americans, chooses to pass among the WASPs."

"Keanu Reeves."

"Tom Hanks."

"Steve and Joe Perry."

"Yup."

Lilly charges the couch in the next room and launches herself in the air.

"This sucks."

"You need to get back in a band," says Em after a long pause. "You were never hurting for lovers, then."

"Get As Malcriadas back together?"

"Nah, start something new."

"Nothing sadder than an aging rocker."

"What the hell does 'malcriada' even mean?"

"After all these years, you don't know? What kind of a Portuguese are you?"

"Not a good one, clearly. It's one of those words we heard growing up like 'corisco.' I get the general sense of it, but I don't know what it means exactly."

"'Corisco,' that's funny. I don't have a clear sense of what that one means either, but 'malcriada' can mean a few things depending on how it's used. Usually it refers to a naughty or bratty child. It can also mean insolent, crude, or ill-bred. Something like that."

"I like it. The Insolent. That was us, alright."

"I always liked The Ill-bred, myself. Put the onus on our parents."

"That too." We went silent, both looking over at Lil who stopped helicopter spinning for a moment when she saw us looking. "What?" she said.

"Nothing, baby."

"Mom, if we had a dog, could we name her Poop?"

"No."

"Why not? It's funny because dogs poop outside. We could say Poop just took a poop."

"Ok, enough of the potty language."

"But it's funny."

"Only to little kids."

"Then why is Auntie Em laughing." I look over to see Em trying to stifle a laugh.

"You're not helping," I say to Em.

"Ok, how about we call her Sweaty, instead?" asks Lilly.

"Fine, Sweaty, fine."

"Then can we get a dog?"

"You fell right into that setup," says Em.

"Nice try, nice try. No, we cannot have a dog. Go watch your show." Lilly takes off. God, that kid is clever. "What am I going to do, Em?"

"What about therapy?"

"Did it."

"Didn't help?"

"Nope. Ian refused to go back after the second meeting."

"Fuck."

"I wish."

Em laughs. My coffee is cold.

I really should have known from the start. Ian and I had been together for almost three months before we finally went to bed. I thought it was charming. He's playing hard to get, I told myself.

He's taking his time, I thought. He wants it to be right. Everyone else wants to have sex right away. They don't much care who you are. They don't want to waste time getting to know you until they've decided if you are worth fucking. When we do it, I thought, it's going to be special. But it wasn't. He was stiff and awkward as if he had never done it before though he assured me he had. He'd kiss me back but it always felt like he was doing me a favor. He was robotic, like his programming had been designed by a person who had read about sex but never done it himself.

"You could move to Japan?"

"How would that help?"

"A quarter of Japanese ages 30-40 are virgins."

"That can't be true."

"It is. Their population numbers are low."

"What is happening over there?"

"Not sure, but as the biggest producer of porn in the world, I guess the boys are all enamored of these impossible manga chicks with tits so big they defy conventional physics. They don't know what to do with real women. They have these services for men where they can rent a girl for a brief time, and not for sex. They're not prostitutes. These girls are for practicing things like being alone with a woman or talking to a woman. I saw a documentary."

"Sounds sad."

"Not sure it's worse than Tinder and that swipe sex thing people do now."

"Or dick pics."

"Gross."

"What about Japanese women?"

"They aren't any better off. There are similar services for women to rent boyfriends and go out on practice dates. No sex allowed either. They literally do things like go shopping together and hold hands."

"Why does that sound so good to me right now? I guess if I'm not going to get any, I might as well be around an entire country that's not getting any."

"The documentary also featured a Japanese woman who invented something she calls a solo wedding where you go through all the stupid nonsense of a wedding but don't marry anyone."

"They marry themselves?"

"Yes."

"Sounds horrible, well, the wedding part, but I guess there are worse things than marrying yourself. I'm basically married to myself as it is."

When Ian and I started dating, I'd clutch him to me and he'd let me, but he did not clutch back. I was aware of all this but I ignored it. No, that's not accurate; I liked it. My other lovers were eager. I liked this about them too. I love to be seduced, who doesn't? This couldn't have been any more different. If I hadn't known that he loved me, he said so, anyway, I probably would have lost interest and stopped pursuing him. Sometimes that is best, better than pretending it's going well, but I liked his cold determination, making me do the work, making me be in charge. At least I liked it at first. He was so commanding in real life, but now I realize he commanded respect by being impenetrable, unreadable, unlikable even. I assumed it would change as he mellowed with age. But he never did. Eventually he started avoiding me completely.

And then he landed the job; Lilly followed shortly after and that was it. Almost a decade in an interminable instant.

"Maybe he's Ace," says Em seriously.

"Maybe," I say, not having considered this option before. "Now, I feel bad," I say, truthfully. He could be Ace, but if he is, he's never said so. I think if he is, we can come to a compromise that will work for both of us. I'm willing to try anything, but since he won't talk to me about it, and since he pretends that there is nothing wrong with our relationship, I can only assume it is something else. "I sometimes hope he has a lover on the side."

"Not likely," says Em.

"No, not at all."

"Why don't you just ask him? Many people have open marriages these days."

"He would never go for it."

"Are you sure?"

"He's oddly jealous."

"But that's not fair. He can't have it both ways."

"He wouldn't be the first."

"Or the last, but you can't go on like this. Can you?"

"What can I do? I have a family. I can't just leave him. I don't even have a job, and I haven't worked in years."

"You wouldn't be the first."

"Or the last. But I don't want that kind of life for Lil. Broken homes do so much damage."

"But you know dead marriages aren't that much better. They could be worse."

"Our marriage isn't dead, yet. Some of it works. What we have works, in its way. It's just that we're more like ..."

"Roommates."

"Yes."

"Ask for a hall pass. You don't know what he'll say."

"What if he says no? ... What if he says yes?"

—

EM
DASH

9

I am watching the last of the old funerals. Every cop in town showed up in uniform, even the honor guard with their perfect white gloves. A band came and played a dirge. They arrived with a pair of tubas, a bass drum, a trombone, some wind players, and a man whose touch on the cymbals was so light and his face so serene it appeared he could already see the other side. And, of course, what remained of the old ladies of the village, already old when I was a child, wondering who might be left to send them away when their time came. These Azoreans of the New World don't express their sorrow in mirth or drunkenness, nor with wild or professional weeping but by being more obdurate than death itself, by waiting in a silence so grim and black clad that death stalks by in fear of their sternness.

Some kind of odd substitution has occurred in my mind. I cannot seem to process the word for grandmother. I am not sure why this other word, why "mangueira," why it insists upon itself as people offer their condolences: "I am so sorry for your mangueira." "Your mangueira is in a better place." "God has called your mangueira to him." It is one of the many absurdities that pop into your mind as you beat back the terror of a world containing one fewer person who loves you. And so mangueira, mangueira, mangueira like an invocation. Mangueira is not Spanish, which is *manguera*, is not the English word for hose. The hose is something the neighbors use to fill their pools, or lubricate the Slip 'N Slide, or feed the sprinkler that saturates more sidewalk than lawn. Mangueira isn't hose. Mangueira is grandfather, is avô (home for the weekend from the sweatshop that would eventually kill him when you were nine) watering his lawn like prayer, like the closest he'd ever come to god was in loving every petal of grass completely, with absolute attention and without prejudice. Mangueira is grandmother, is avó, is the plastic-runner and metal taste of water when school is out for summer and you need a drink but can't enter the house because she (usually the surest place for love) will beat you within an inch of your life with her chinela if you track dirt on her freshly mopped linoleum. Mangueira is water, is an interrogation of the road you took when you left town because it is only a place to die in, a place of silence without repose.

My parents are at the head of the receiving line. We are nearly 20 deep—a small generation sired from a much larger one—and I am at the very end, putting as many people as possible between them and me. All night I have to deal with sideward glances from all the old ladies for not being in my proper place as the oldest grandchild—just more proof that I am unkind, disrespectful, a bad daughter, a malcriada. But I don't care. I am here for my grandmother. I am not here for them. I am not here for my parents, and I am getting out of town the second my beautiful avó is laid to rest and going to visit Gilgamesh and her new baby in Providence. Plus, every time I get too close to the corpse—because that body is not my grandmother—I want to laugh in that way one laughs when everything has gone completely wrong and nothing to be done.

I leave her body to its private silence. A body in silence breaks the devil's laughter and is an interrogation of that laughter. My avó used to say, "O diabo é sempre bom para rir, mas ele é o único a rir," which means, "The devil is always good for a laugh, but he is the only one laughing." Do these somewhat familiar mourners wonder what it's like to laugh without speaking, to take from a muttering of shoulders a measure of the wreck of us, like a dare to keep living? Is it, like this? Like an irony that unravels? Or is it, like this? Like a road that is water, that buckles like a parched tongue, a tongue that breaks where the rocks are deep and then too quickly shallow? My tongue is shallow and does not reach like displacement in a mouth of water. I cannot speak when they shake my hands. I cannot speak to explain. My mouth is water but not a body I want to drown in—a body that buries what I thought to share. It is a breath from below that cracks a road that isn't water but still holds the memory of you like rivers are said to do, like grandmothers are said to do. I am sad sometimes to think I shall never be buried in the family plot in Notre Dame Cemetery—a cemetery full of my people with a French name. When my time comes, no one will water the earth newly-turned, no mangueira to bind me to the land—my body an interrogation that pretends not to be an interrogation.

THE GREAT GILGAMESH

10

SOMERSET 1995

As summers always do, this one ends far too quickly. Only parents think summers linger. September rolls in just in time for us to leave for our respective colleges. I leave in the morning. We know we'll see each other in a few months, but we have never been apart for longer than a couple of days, a week at most, since we can remember. All of our schools are within driving distance of one another, but since we aren't allowed to have cars on campus and are too broke to afford to take a bus, we know we won't see each other until winter break. There's been an inconsolable restlessness about us for weeks, the kind of restlessness that comes from facing the fact that nothing can be done except to get through. We are out of time—a fact so naked in its sharpness we are all cut and bleeding. I can't help but feel guilty because though I don't want to leave my friends, I am really excited about what is to come. I've been waiting my whole life to leave for college, not go to college but leave for college.

"Let's go to the school yard," I suggest.

"Why?"

"Because ... I don't know why. Let's just get out of here. I need to walk." Em and Manny agree. Does everyone do this, go for one last ride on the swings, take a few last—surprisingly bone-jangling—jumps at the swing's peak and into the sand that contains more broken glass and cigarette butts than you remember? Manny suggests this little scene we are playing out is probably pretty common.

"Doesn't this feel a little like the scene in *The Wonder Years* where Kevin and Winnie are falling in love after the death of her brother?"

"Oh my god, Em. I was just thinking that."

"She's half Portuguese, you know," I say.

"Who?"

"What do you mean, who? Danica McKellar, that's who."

"She's one of ours? That kicks ass."

"God, I hate how much I love that show."

"Boomer nostalgia—it's not even our past, not our songs, not our war."

"Jeez, Manny."

"You love that show as much as we do."

"I never said I didn't, but it doesn't change what I'm saying. It's all bull crap."

Manny cares about everything. People listen when he speaks, his seriousness apparent and honest. Em, on the other hand, could hit you between the eyes with a brick and you'd thank her for it.

"Well, it's no *Who's the Boss?*" says Em.

"Yeah, but what is?" Manny says laughing. "'Yo, Angela!' Is he one of ours?"

"No, he's Italian-American."

"Darn."

I have been in love with Em since the fifth grade. It was in that year I realized the difference. My love was not of the

innocent kind, though it was not sex yet. It isn't fun being
in love with one of your best and oldest friends. There she
is, always and ever in front of you, daring you to take a sip. I
have never made a move on my Em—I wouldn't even know
how—but it's been painfully obvious how far my feelings go.
And I'm not the only one. I've never met anyone who could
resist her. If she wasn't so kind, she could have enslaved us
all to her every whim, but she never did—with her bobbed
haircut and her sundresses, her eyeliner and doc martins. I
can't tell if she suspects me or not. I've noticed Em pretends
not to know things sometimes.

"We could test it," suggests Manny.

"Test what?"

"We go to all the elementary schools in town and see how
many of the swing sets are peopled with kids too old to be on
the swings."

"Sounds simple enough."

"I'll draw up a table."

Manny loves drawing graphs and tables, and he always
has an experiment running. When he was a kid, that usually
meant corrosive chemicals from his father's garage eating away
at various materials—Styrofoam cups, tins, and coffee cans
carefully labeled and lining his work bench. It was straight
mad science but with clear method. What would catch fire,
what explode? What was the melting point of fishing line?
How much weight could it hold before breaking? He won
every science fair at school. It wasn't even close. When other
kids' clubhouses were nothing more than a platform in a tree,
his would be a many-storied affair with working doors and
multiple escape routes. It's just how he is built. He loves devis-
ing plans and schemes, loves isolating the one variable that

will hopefully reveal truths hidden under the chaos of the every day. Manny obsesses about what other people are really thinking. Do they think the same thoughts we do? Are people more or less the same or is there a huge range with only the illusion of sameness? He didn't know and wasn't sure which was preferable. Were things better now or worse? Were people more or less decent or were we the evil dimension? Manny felt the most boring interpretation of the multiverse model was the evil dimension idea. Given a concept that posits all possible consequences for our choices, the best we can do is one antithetical dimension where a goatee indicates your opposite. But what if we are the evil dimension? Look at the facts! Given what we know about our world, the notion that we are the good dimension seems flimsy at best.

At the park, we have to hitch our legs up a few inches in order to pump the swings properly. It's not exactly natural or comfortable. We haven't played here since club houses and bologna sandwiches crunchy with beach sand. Oddly, our band's very first gig was at this schoolyard. The summer after our freshman year in high school, the PTA organized a little carnival and our music teacher got us the gig. He was a terrifying man because we all wanted desperately to impress him. At 50, which to us seemed perilously old—positively Malthusian—he showed us that life was far from over. Late in life, he decided he wanted to get his doctorate. Then he decided he wanted to get a black belt in judo—both of which he achieved. More than liking us, we wanted him to take us seriously because he was serious and we didn't know many people who were serious about anything worth being serious about. Our parents cared about their lawns, church, and tele-vised sports. And those were the good parents, the ones who

because they were poor or because they were immigrants—
like my parents—didn't act like selfish children. Em's parents,
on the other hand, would disappear for weeks at a time and
not even tell Em where they were going. As much as I'd love
for my parents to leave me the house for a week, we could tell
it bothered Em a lot, though she never said much about them
one way or another.

We had no idea what they did. We had never met them
and she would not tell us anything. I have known Em all my
life and have never spoken to either of her parents, not really.
If we came to pick her up, she'd be on the front porch waiting because she didn't want us to come to the door. We were
forbidden from calling the house. When we were twelve or
thirteen, Manny and I decided to call just to hear what her parents sounded like. We pretended to be selling magazines with
silly titles like *Twig and Two Berries* and *Refrigerators Monthly*.
When Em found out, she was furious and didn't speak to us for
the rest of that year, which in junior high is like a decade. We
were just goofing around; we had no idea she would totally go
off the rails. I'd never seen her that mad before or since. It's safe
to say that Manny and I never did that again. We respected her
privacy and steered clear of the topic. She never said she hated
them. She just never spoke of them, as if she had been born
through asexual reproduction. Manny says Em is sui generis,
whatever the hell that means. Sometimes I wonder if Manny is
just making this shit up. It's not like I have any way of checking.
What am I going to do, go to the library? Not likely.

The day of the carnival we played the few songs we knew
on the back of a flatbed truck they rented as a stage to an
audience of little children, parents, and a handful of our school
buddies. It wasn't exactly Lollapalooza. We'd only been a band

for like six months at the time. We weren't good. I mean, we were fifteen. In all fairness, we were forgettable, but we were feeling pretty good about ourselves after we played—until the next performer got on stage, that is. His name was Scott. He was unassuming, a shortish, blond-haired boy a few years older than us. He got on stage alone with his acoustic guitar. When he started to sing, I wanted to rush on stage and squeeze the life out of him. I wanted to pummel him to death. I wanted to abduct him. I wanted to sell all my worldly possessions, shave my head, and travel the land spreading his word. I wanted to start a war in his name. I wanted to write an epic poem about the mythical founding of his country: Scotland. Nothing else would do. I had been waiting for these songs all my life, and I didn't even know it. They were inevitable. I knew it the second he played "Lemonade" and "Tepid," songs few people in the outside world would ever hear, each one as if it had always just been there. They were simple tunes, but they had everyone in the small audience in his power, not that he seemed to notice, which was so sexy.

His name was Scott and he was the lead singer of a band we would come to love called Blair's Carriage. Scott with eyes closed; Scott with cigarette jammed in the head of his guitar. Scott singing about a girl named Lori. Scott so lovely and perfect this tiny town could barely hold him. After he finished his set, we went looking for him. We didn't know what we were going to say because we would have said anything. We didn't know what we were going to do because we would have done anything. When we finally spotted him, he was in one of these very swings next to a pretty pixie of a girl. I knew she must be Lori of "Lori's Curb." I wanted it to be Lori. I needed it to be Lori. I just knew she would be something. She would have to be too much or never mind. And I was half right. As I approached closer, I finally got a clear look at her. It was Em, of course. She could easily be the girl of his songs since to me she was every girl in every song. When we asked her about Scott, she simply said he was nice. "Nice?" Nice! I couldn't think of a less revealing word than "nice." I don't know what I was expecting her to say; I guess I was hoping that his specialness would be revealed in his talk, in his gestures, in his very closeness, but if it did, Em wasn't sharing. All my life I thought talent was enough to get us through, but it isn't. It always falls short somehow.

Back in the present, we list gently in our swings, trying to say what will not allow itself to be said as the sun lazes on the horizon. The little school house at the top of the hill remains closed for the summer. Over there is the door where we clapped erasers in fourth grade. Over there, the field where we schooled the boys at Muckle—a game someone made up with no scoring and no way to win, where the only goal was to tackle the person holding the football. Over there, the kickball court and the steps we used as a stage for our improvised dramatizations and puppet shows. The school grounds were bordered by woods where we picked wild blackberries so tart it was a dare to eat them, and where Devil's Rock was hidden behind the meagerest of coverings, where junior high kids carry on the timeless tradition of smoking cigarettes stolen from their parents or sharing a lone lukewarm beer they hoped no one would notice missing from the second fridge in the garage. Devil's Rock is where so many of us had our first terrible kisses, which isn't far from the pond full of small frogs and leaches that nearly swallowed Manny one winter, when he became Frost Heaves Emmanuel. All so long ago. By tomorrow, we'll be packing minivans while our mothers talk without stopping and our fathers clean newly-emptied rooms in determined and shaky silence. We'll pack. Our mothers will talk. Our fathers will clean. Life will begin.

FROST HEAVES EMMANUEL

11

CHICAGO 2015

Fifteen years under fluorescent lights walking the universally brown-flecked asbestos tiles. Fifteen years in classrooms by turns too hot or too cold, with windows locked against light and air. I get older but the students stay the same. I know the fact of this. I don't need a double-blind study to prove it to myself, and yet, somehow, I can't quite grasp the problem. It's a strange thing to find elusive. I remind myself over and over that these are not the same students I had last semester and the semester before that, that it is the first time they are seeing the material, that it isn't a sinister plot to entrap me in a never-ending eternal return. As the years pass, the energy once spent refining the class has been shifted to sustaining what I can only think of as selective amnesia. The more I forget, the better I am. Experience, it seems, has a price tag too.

My own college essays provide concrete and incontrovertible proof contradicting the very powerful illusion that I was somehow better, smarter, or more advanced in my thinking than my students. The illusion of early mastery is endemic to teaching—and probably to most professions. My papers show I had the exact same strengths and weaknesses, the same desires to write papers about "The Big Game," "Abortion," and "Gun

77

Control." But my college papers also prove a second but equally important point. They demonstrate that if you keep at it, you can and will improve. Corny, I know, but the evidence is no less compelling in this case. How much improvement is a completely different question I cannot answer. What I do know is that my college writing shows no especial talent, though I was a very diligent and successful pupil. I tell my students that if I can do it, anyone can—and I have evidence to back up my claims.

What I don't say is that mastery comes at the behest of terrible hunger, a sickness I see in some of my students. It is a hunger that has known starvation in its past and is utterly unable to forget that fact even in times of plenty—maybe especially in times of plenty. I was not aware how much it could reach through my defenses, how I showed this desperation even in what I thought was a neutral face. My serious face, apparently, is dour, like I am judging you even when it is quite clear I am not. When Gomez and I were in college, we took one class together, only one. We were way too competitive, so we decided to take an astronomy course our senior year because it was a discipline we both liked but had nothing to do with our majors. I don't know if it was the first or second class, but during a lecture, Gomez looked over and mouthed, "What's wrong?" Nothing was wrong. I had no idea what he was talking about. After class, Gomez told me I had a look of such intense disgust on my face that he thought I was angry about something the professor had said, which couldn't have been further from the truth. I liked the professor, especially when he took us to the roof to use the telescope—a set piece from every 80s sitcom I ever loved but never experienced in real life. I asked for a telescope every Christmas and birthday and never got one. College was like this for me, something almost too wonderful to be real—even the drudgery of homework assignments and group projects where I did all the work. During my college years, I kept waiting to awaken into a reduced world, as if I was merely window shopping, as if it was one of those terrible yearning dreams. Is this the grimace I've been showing my teachers and my students all these years? Is this the face that launched countless ships and burned the topless towers of Ilium? How does he frown? Is it, like this? Like a plane of stone? A sheet of rust? Or is it, like this? Like a bounced check, a broken promise?

Being a part-time instructor makes me wonder why I ever wanted to be a teacher in the first place, though it has been the only thing I have ever wanted to do since I was a child. It's respectable. It's clean. It won't break my body like the textile mills did to my parents, or so I thought. But as an adjunct, I don't make a living wage. They don't tell you this part when you are young, that you can get a fraction of a dream, just enough of it to keep you bound forever to it but never enough to set you free to live your life. I teach four classes at several different institutions—and that's on a good semester when I can get the work. I have over a hundred written papers to grade per assignment out of four major paper assignments. I spend more time on the train going from school to school than I do in the classroom. I teach a full-time course load for less than $20,000 a year, with no insurance or job security. If it weren't for Gomez, I wouldn't be able to survive on this money. I'd have been forced to abandon this course years ago, and maybe that would have been the best thing for me, though what else I'd be able to do for money is beyond me.

After five years or so of adjunct teaching, Gomez realized there was no future in academia—that he had somehow been tainted, that he gave off some kind of pheromone stink that employers were picking up on, so he went to work for a nonprofit. It was not bad work, but it wasn't what he dreamed of doing. The long slow commute to work was driving him crazy—a closed road at both ends, a powerful tool of erosion. Like so many people in our generation, good people trapped between the monster-sized generations of the Baby Boomers and the Millennials, he could not find a way to grab hold of the life that was promised him by his professors. We all fall for failure. It's like marrying young and promising never to change, promising like a dare against the universe, like a needle in a field of needles awaiting a single thread. Being a failure is a pair of fingerless gloves. They look warm but the important part never quite stops the freezing nor its necessity to touch. For a couple months he could barely get off the couch. He forced himself to work, forced himself to eat, to shower. Nothing came easy. He'd lay around all weekend, saying little and staring off into space. Nothing I did helped. He was far beneath a layer of permafrost. I was terrified. I had been below and I knew how hard it was to come back.

When we were grad students, we had our hearts set on four-year colleges. Our teachers defined success very narrowly, though they had no idea how much the job market had changed in 30 years. We bought it wholesale at the time, but now I would take any teaching job at all. Actually, I enjoy working at community colleges even more than universities—not that the junior college jobs are any easier to land, it turns out. At least the students aren't entitled little brats. These were not students who thought you owed them an A just because they came to class. Far from it. To be fair, though, when you charge students four or five times the tuition their parents paid, you better expect at least some grade inflation. In 1995, a large, research one, land-grant institution cost around $10,000 a year in-state, with room, board, and meal plan included. These same institutions now cost upwards of $40,000. Most of my community college students are so thankful for any kind of positive attention that it hurts to realize how little I can actually do for them. They believe in me, but belief has nothing to do with it. As I so often tell them, the universe doesn't care what you believe.

And Gomez and I were so tired of living in tiny, one-bedroom apartments—all the appliances worn and battered and barely in working order like our parents' desiccated and abraded bodies—bodies of jagged glacial ice. We still had the same kit furniture we bought in 2005 for our first apartment. It was mostly wood glue and wishing by this point, not really furniture at all. But Gomez's sacrifice eventually paid off. He quickly worked his way up through the ranks to become an administrator at the YMCA's national headquarters. The salary is good. He helps people in his way, though not in the way he'd like. I want to be worthy of his sacrifice. And, if I am honest, I want to stay ahead of the next storm. Though Gomez has not had any relapses, his slow sinking dissatisfaction frightens me. I never know when the frost will heave, when what is buried deep will rise to the surface to possess him again, like when I went beneath the ice as a child—a story Gomez makes me tell him over and over like he can tell some part of me remains there even now. When the pavement breaks in winter, I can feel the vacant goggle eyes of the drowned ones on me, waiting for a body to take, waiting to come back up for air. All the drowned children find the deep does not sleep so easy. And then they yearn to go back under. Sometimes, those eyes blaze at me from my students, from my husband, from my mirror.

THE GREAT GILGAMESH

12

Summer break arrives and we finally have some serious time to hang out like we used to. The first year of college is behind us now, and we can get back to our real lives. It would already be a good day if that was all that we had in the world, but today we huddle around the radio waiting to hear one of our songs played during prime time on 95.5 WBRU—the alternative rock station out of Providence. It is the same station where I heard "Smells Like Teen Spirit" for the first time one night in 1991 and knew exactly what I wanted to do with my life—the same station that introduced me to "Even Flow," "Cornflake Girl," "Doll Parts," "Last Goodbye," and "Would?" Though we've had a couple songs from our EP "Drunk on Water" played on the local college station really late at night (because the DJ is the older sister of a school friend), this is on a totally different level. Better still, they were going to play a song from our new album, which we barely managed to record over winter break. I admit after that first rehearsal back in December, I was ready to walk away. I had never been so close to quitting the band before. I had been counting the days until break, counting the days until the semester was over and we'd all be together again, counting the days when we could lock ourselves in our studio and rock out like we used to—and with the first good drummer since Jessie. I practiced almost every day. I had a whole bunch of new songs ready to go once we were done recording the full album, titled Common Weeds. And then they slap me in the face, like no one gave a shit about the band at all. Like I had to hold everybody's hand all the damn time, as usual. I mean, how hard is it to practice? We had a couple days to get it together and I didn't think we'd pull it off, but somehow we did after a few harrowing days and nights. Today makes me happy I did not quit. Never been so happy to be wrong in my life.

A week ago, we had participated in an annual battle of the bands in Providence called The Rock Hunt, and they were playing singles by bands that had done well in the contest. We didn't win but we did get pretty far. And we weren't going to pretend to be cool about it. This is too big for nonchalance, too amazing for irony, too beyond for pretense. Maybe I am only imagining it, but it feels like everyone in town has their car radios tuned to 95.5, hoping to catch the moment the local kids go on to bigger and better things. It may not be true, but I don't care. Today, it feels like it could actually happen. I don't know how I managed to keep quiet about it for so long, but I wanted the timing to be right. There definitely can be too much of a good thing, and I didn't know how many such moments we'd get in our lives. Everything in its true time. I feared to think too much about it, like I'd bring ruin upon us if I gave into my happiness without a certain amount of restraint. Sometimes it feels like people like us aren't allowed to be happy. Sometimes it feels like the expectation that the universe not dump all over us is too much to ask. We are always on the edge of disaster— the smallest thing a cataclysm. There is no room for error and no place to go if we lose any more ground—only a cliff's edge. We don't have the option of tactical retreat. There is reckless offense and surrender—or annihilation, I guess. But not today, not today. "Today is the greatest / day I've ever known …"

"And here's a tune from Massachusetts's own As Malcriadas called, 'I Will Save Myself.'" We ignore his terrible pronunciation of the band name as the opening notes of my guitar riff cuts through the DJ's patter and strikes us dumb, like being touched by the finger of god itself. Our song is on the airwaves for everyone to hear. Ash loses his cool and begins stomping about restlessly, which causes an avalanche of hugs and high fives and cheering until we realize we are missing it. After a quick bout of shushing, we go back to listening. Brittle silence once again descends on the rehearsal space, which we dubbed Casa Pancada or the House of Blows (bilingual pun intended)—my basement we'd commandeered years ago when my neighbors complained to my parents about us rehearsing in the garage. No one speaks, but we're having a tough time containing the energy in our bodies—feet tap, legs jig, heads bob, lyrics are lipped. In my mind, I can't resist the reenactment in our biopic years from now, memorializing the moment when we knew we were going to make it. Cue the big movie music as better-looking young people huddle around the radio much more stylishly than we are doing at this exact moment, with their profound sense of ease that comes from the absolute certainty of future success, of belonging completely to this side of the Atlantic.

"Epic," says Ash and we nod assent, stupid and rare smiles sticking to our faces. No one knows what to do next. We can't meet each other's eyes. It is simply too much, but I am going to lose my mind if I don't tell them the rest of the news. I stand to address the band.

"Speech, speech, speech," says Manny sarcastically.

"Shut up. Ok, but I do have something to say."

"Shocker," says Ash, as if he wasn't the one who couldn't keep his mouth shut a moment ago.

"I have some more news."

"Fuck yes! Wait, it's good news, right?" asks Ash suddenly suspicious.

"Yes, very good," and I feel every single sigh of relief.

"Are we getting signed by Sub Pop?" jokes Kid, his frilly sleeve nearly chewed to bits from anxiety.

"Well, no ... not Sub Pop ..."

"Dang it," he laughs and someone titters.

"But ... I heard back from Big Noise Records in New York, and they have accepted one of our songs for their next compilation CD."

"Holy crap!"

"What!"

"Seriously?"

"And ..." I say, trying to quiet them a little.

"And what," they all say in comic unison.

"They liked the album so much they want to sign us."

And nothing. No one makes a sound. All their mouths are stuck open for a second that stretches out to eternity.

"Oh, my, fucking, god!" everyone seems to say suddenly, though not everyone does so out loud. We lose ourselves one more time in the jumping and stomping and screaming and stammering that is the only way we can figure to get through the moment. We have no previous experience to draw on and so have to invent a way on the spot. For a second all the gas stations, factories, and pizza joints fade away and the town recedes in the rearview mirror of our biopic scene, the car packed with guitar cases, amps, and drum equipment—hair blowing in the wind as our first hit plays us into the sunset.

"We're signed. We're signed! Holy shit."

"We did it! We did it!" someone yells.

"I can't believe it."

"Now, remember, they're just an indie label," I say.

"Who cares! This is amazing."

"Ok, but there's one last thing."

This is the part I have been dreading. Suddenly, their faces drop, their smiles becoming thin lines, the reality of who they are coming back on them to crush what they all knew had to be too good to be true. It is Ash who speaks it, "Here it comes," he sighs. "I knew there was a catch." They were feeling the knife edge of their lives again, where everything comes only at the cost of blood—and not a little.

"No, it's not like that … exactly."

"Well, what is it, exactly?" Ash only has one way of dealing with disappointment. He goes straight to full asshole, which means he is an asshole almost all the time, but I don't blame him this time.

"They're going to re-release our album … and they want us to support it."

"Ok," says Ash confused.

"I don't get it," someone says.

"By going on tour," I say carefully.

No one speaks.

"To Europe."

I had planned to say this with excitement. I had planned to roll it into the celebration, to include it as a part of the good news, but I couldn't force myself to fake it. If we were other kids, real American kids, that is exactly how it would go, but I knew what it would mean to a bunch of kids who had never been anywhere or done anything. Reality sat among us now, smugly taking up the lion's share of the beat-to-hell couch we are sitting on like a jumble of puzzle pieces. We needed to be touching each other almost all the time. We'd pile onto one couch even if there were more places to sit. We'd clown-car everywhere rather than take several cars. We even established a club that heightened our notoriety in high school dubbed the WBC or Warm Butt Club, which was nothing more than group napping in one bed. No shenanigans were allowed, but that didn't stop our peers from gossiping: "Hey, Jealousy." Now the magic couch is inducing mild bouts of claustrophobia, and people begin to move out into the space of the room. Getting signed is what we all want. Getting signed sounds good. Getting signed is rock-and-roll and the movies, but getting signed also means business, means money. We feared money. Big Noise Records will want to make money. We will have to sell ourselves. Obviously, we had always dreamed of touring someday, but in the face of it now, we are little children. We are afraid. Touring Europe? Sure, sounds easy, but I'd only ever been to the Azores and that was with my parents. That's as close as I'd ever come to anywhere and the Azores are a group of islands in the middle of the Atlantic Ocean. Islands lost to humanity until the Portuguese blundered onto them in the 15th century. I've never been anywhere alone and neither has anyone else. I am exactly 19, and only 19. The moment is lost; our song is forgotten.

"Well," Ash finally says, "we knew we would have to do this, guys. Right? Isn't this the goal? We're signed. We're going on tour," he says trying to recapture the excitement of a moment ago, and I am grateful to Ash for the second time today. It has to be some kind of record.

"My parents will never let me go," says Kid sadly. He's still in high school, still a minor.

"How long's the tour?"

"Just for the summer."

"Oh," says Ash much more brightly. "Fuck it, then. Would you rather work some shit job and live with your parents or go on tour? I mean, it's not even close."

"They did say that if Europe went well, they'd want us to do Japan and if that went well, we'd return and do the States." Kid looks doubly devastated. Why can't I keep my mouth shut? They didn't need to know that now? I'm like that person who hides behind honesty in order to put others down. Feche a bouca. Keep your mouth closed.

"Hey, c'mon guys. Seriously? This is great news! Kid, we'll find a way. We'll talk to your parents. I don't know. Why are we all scared all of a sudden? That's what it means to be a band. I mean, are we just playing around here or are we serious? Are we just big talk? Scott went to California. Now, it's our turn."

"Ash's right. We can't launch a music career from Somerset," I say.

"But Scott went alone," says Em. "Blair's Carriage did not go with him."

"Are we just a bunch of poseurs?"

"It's not that simple."

"It's just for the summer, Em," says Manny.

"Look, whether this tour goes well or not, we have to move to L.A. at some point. We can't stay here." I guess I was hoping that everyone else would be excited and, for once, I could gather courage from them. It is exhausting having to be cheerleader, manager, and life coach. The tragedy of the makers. No one will do for you what they fully expect you to

89

do for them. I hate being in charge. "What do you think?" I ask, hopefully.

"I'm no poseur. I'm in," says Ash.

"Manny?"

"I'm in if my boyfriend can come."

"Good … wait, what? Boyfriend? Since when?" I ask, eyes goggling out of my skull.

"Ooh, what's his name?" asks Kid in a mocking tone. I think he has a crush on Manny.

"Gomez Addams"

"Gomez Addams?" asks Kid, not letting it go.

"His last name is Gomes, Francisco Gomes, but his teachers don't know how to pronounce it, so he became Gomez."

"Oh," we manage to say in unison again. If only people understood that Portuguese is not Spanish.

"Holy shit! You little vixen," I say.

"Can we please get back on topic?" asks Ash, suddenly the responsible one.

"I'm in," I say, "but I want to hear more about this Gomez character later."

"But of course."

"Kid?"

"If you can convince my parents, I'm so totally and completely in."

"Tell your parents you want to spend the summer in Portugal with your vavó, then we'll come get you."

"Could work," says Kid dubiously.

"Em?"

I knew she'd be a problem. Em never imagined we'd get this far. To be perfectly honest, she doesn't think we are all that good. She's never said so, but it's pretty clear to me. Em is a restless soul; she can't give herself fully to anything. She's always chasing the next thing, always looking for the rush of novelty and running the second she senses a door closing or border shrinking. I could never understand it myself. I've been feeling her pull away since winter break; no, since long before that. I think I might have sensed it at the end of last summer. She was already gone; we just didn't know it. I doubted she'd do the tour, but I'm not sure I can do this without her. I need her with me. I need the whole band or this is just too difficult. The story is wrong without her. It'll be Jessie all over again, but worse. "Em?"

"I need to think."

"Oh, c'mon. Seriously?" says Ash. "You're going to fuck this up for us?"

"I'm not fucking anything up for anyone."

"We're not going to get many chances like this. For some of us, this might be our only chance."

"That's not my fault, is it?"

"In this case, yes it is!"

"Ash, please," I say.

"It's one summer!"

"No, it's not one summer. It's this summer, then I'm missing school because I have to go to Japan. Then, I'm missing the rest of the year because we have to tour the U.S. And yet, after all that, we will likely still not make it. So, there's another tour, another country. Same old shit, different day. Suddenly, I'm 40 years old, and I have no education, no job, no nothing. All I have is a bunch of stories about all the shit hotels I stayed in and crappy bars I played when I was young. No, thank you."

"You know, there's always someone to fuck shit up for everyone else. I hope your life amounts to shit, Em." Ash grabs his ubiquitous John Cusack trench coat, punches the wall like a dumbass, and storms out of the rehearsal space, all the excitement ruined, his future looking small and bleak all over again.

"Ash, she didn't say no," I say to his retreating back.

"Em, this really isn't a difficult decision. You know Ash is right," says Manny in that matter of fact way that can sometimes feel patronizing. "You know you want to go."

"Um, yes, it is a difficult decision, Manny. You don't get to tell me what I feel."

"I'm not. I just think you'll regret not doing this."

"Right, because what you care about is my wellbeing. You know this has nothing to do with what I want."

"That's not fair," says Manny. "When have I ever not cared about your wellbeing?"

"You care so long as it doesn't inconvenience your plans. You're no better than Ash. At least he has the courage to say it out loud," and it is Em's turn to stomp out of the studio.

"Em! C'mon, Em! You know that's not true. How could you say that?" asks Manny, a look of panic on his face that says he realizes too late that the world as he knows it is now gone forever. He looks at me and I shrug and pretend not to know. Now who's pretending not to know things? I'm the Girl Who Doesn't Know. Oh Em. This song is for you. Listen to it imagining you. Does it catch like a hook or linger on the air as if held by the elbow? Is it someone calling your name? How does it sound? Is it, like this? Like a smudge of geek-girl red lipstick on a tooth? Or is it, like this? A claxon, a warning?

FROST HEAVES EMMANUEL

13

CHICAGO 2015

"Gomez? Gomez?"

"I'm in the bathroom."

"Still? What's going on in there?"

"My ass."

"I assumed that much."

"Very funny. No, my ass. It's bleeding."

"That's not good. A lot?"

"I don't know. What's a lot?"

"Drops, stream, deluge?"

"Drops."

"Are they bright red?" I ask.

"Are you Googling?"

"Obviously. Answer the question."

"Red," he says.

"Not black?"

"No, red."

"Does it feel like pooping glass?"

"Yes, exactly."

"Anal fissure."

"It hurts."

"Told you to go easy with those beads."

"Go big or go home, that's what I always say," jokes Gomez. "All are punished."

"Damn it. Entertain me. I'm going to be here for a while. Ow, ow, ow."

"The romance will never die."

"I know, baby. Who's got it better than us? Entertain me. Please."

"Ok, ok. Give me a second," I say, trying to come up with something to distract Gomez from his predicament. "Did you read the article I sent you about the Church of England?"

"No."

"You never read anything I send you."

"I'm sorry, I always forget."

"Likely story," I say teasing since this is a fake argument we have all the time. I don't really care if he reads the things I send him and he knows it.

"So what's going down with the Church of England?"

"Well, it sold all its stock in a British oil company because they wanted to drill for oil in Virunga National Park?"

"That's amazing."

"Are you being sarcastic?"

"No. Imagine if American religious institutions acted this way?"

"I know, even the Pope is trashing the rich."

"I never thought I'd like anything a pope had to say. God, this hurts," says Gomez.

"You ok?"

"Yes, keep talking. It helps."

"Ok. Um, do you remember my student, Lovemore? I ran into him today on campus. He's getting his doctorate now. Can you believe that?"

"Lovemore Dick? How could I forget?"

"Is that the only part of the story you remember?"

"Hard thing to forget," says Gomez.

"It's pronounced "'Love-a-more,' anyway."

"I know. I know."

"Names matter," I say more vehemently than I had intended. "You leave my unfortunately-named student alone. Without him I would have quit teaching years ago."

"Ok, ok. Sorry. What about Lovemore?" he asks, pronouncing it properly.

"He told me today the story of how he came to the States. It's horrible. Before coming to Chicago, he had lived in Virunga. Well, lived, I don't know. He was hiding out. Soldiers had massacred his family right in front of him. Congo was a mess in the 90's and there were lots of refugees in Virunga."

"Why?"

"Civil war. Anyway, he tells me this crazy story about how he ended up living near some chimps, and he remembered the day we read a short essay in class by Jane Goodall and the chimps in Gombe. Chimps are extremely territorial, so Goodall describes how she has to inch closer and closer over a long period of time to allow the chimps to get accustomed to having her in their territory, and amazingly they eventually accept her as one of the females of the troop."

"Is that the proper collective noun? Troop?"

"Think so."

"Ok, how about this," says Gomez. "Did you know that Curious George isn't a monkey? The Man in the Yellow Hat always calls him a little monkey but he clearly isn't a monkey. He has no tail and his front legs are longer than his back legs, which is consistent with chimp physiognomy. Curious George is a chimp."

"Lies. So many lies. So, Lovemore tells me today that while he was in Virunga, the chimps would come and peek at him, and eventually they started to steal food he left unguarded. One young chimp would throw anything he could get his hands on at Lovemore, and then he'd laugh if he managed to hit him. Lovemore said he spent many of his days watching them play."

"Isn't it weird that Chimps make nests?"

"Are you Googling?"

"Yes, I'm fact checking."

"Dick. Yes, they make nests kind of like birds. He said they used sticks to make a kind of basket in the trees. He saw them use sticks as ladders to climb especially tall trees and to eat ants and termites."

"Chimps are so badass."

"I'm just glad they didn't tear his arms off and beat him to death with them."

"Right?"

"Isn't that what people always say?"

"I wonder where they got that idea from. I mean, are there bands of one-armed scientists and zookeepers going around maligning the reputation of the chimp?"

"Apropos, did you see the new *Planet of the Apes*?"

"Nope."

"They just rebooted it. I never liked the original, nor the Marky Mark version, but this one looks good."

"Marky Mark and the Funky Bunch. That's some funny shit."

"Want to watch it tonight?"

"I'm amenable if you ever get your butt off the toilet."

"Oh god, why did you remind me? It does feel like I'm pooping broken glass. Do you think I have colon cancer?"

"If you're so worried about it, go see a doctor. You're almost 40. You should probably go anyway."

"I don't want to."

"You're going to be a baby about this?"

"The Portuguese have a saying, *You only go to the hospital ...*"

"*When you are ready to die.* Yes, I know that one. Doesn't make it true."

"Butt stuff is personal."

"After what we did last night?"

"Well, I did that with you, not with my doctor."

"What kind of gay man are you?"

"I'm not gay, I'm bi. You of all people should know the difference."

"Ok, ok, I apologize. I was only making a joke. Your sexuality is valid."

"Thank you. What happened with Lovemore?"

"Don't try to distract me."

"I'm not. You're supposed to be distracting me."

"Lovemore lived with chimps and you are afraid of a little gloved finger?"

"Well, unless the chimps were trying to check his prostate, I don't see how the situations are related."

"Can I finish my story?"

"I wish you would."

"One day, Lovemore said he heard the chimps screaming and making a great deal of noise, and he was afraid a poacher or some other predator was attacking them, but it turned out one of the mothers had just given birth. He described how the entire troop seemed to be celebrating the new baby. Some of the other female chimps were attempting to caress it, but the new mother was having none of it."

"He needs to use that story to win some fellowships or something."

"That's exactly what I told him."

"Great minds. Babe? I need toilet paper."

"You're hopeless."

"Love you."

I didn't, however, tell Lovemore (or Gomez) the rest of Goodall's story, which was not in the excerpt. I didn't mention the day she watched Passion and Pom, a mother-daughter team, eat the child of a lesser female and then embrace the half-dead mother as if to say it was just business. And I didn't mention that it wasn't, as Goodall had hoped, an aberration, how she watched from her spot in a baobab tree as they did it again and again. Dominant females protect their positions in the hierarchy too, with sometimes violent results. I couldn't take that story from Lovemore anymore than I could take it from myself. I need Lovemore to make it. I want to say Lovemore saved the day. I want to say I survived in Virunga among the chimps. I want to say it was more than just business.

THE GREAT GILGAMESH

14

PROVIDENCE 2015

When Ian gets home, he'll head straight for the bedroom, but I'm not going to let him get there because once he hits the pillow that will be it for the night. Ian has conquered sleep in a way I never could—my own personal Enkidu. I have been waiting for hours, waiting like a jealous wife for her cheating husband to skulk home or an angry mother for her wayward teen to sneak in the bedroom window reeking of skunk weed and cigarette smoke. It has been a while since I've ambushed him. It's unfair, I know, but there is never a good time with Ian. On weekends, he makes sure never to be around the house for long. If he isn't at work or preparing material for work, he will be running errands. And he doesn't do it in a systematic way. For example, he doesn't make a list and then go out to run all of his errands. He goes out for a cup of coffee and comes back. Then he realizes he needs paperclips, so he'll go to Staples to buy one pack of paperclips. Then the car needs gas, so he's off again. He isn't trying to be efficient, and it's not some innate inability to organize his time properly. Quite the opposite, actually—he is trying to waste as much time as possible. No, not waste (like me he cannot abide waste) he is consuming time—eating it like some dark god. He'll do this all weekend, every weekend. Most days I'm just too tired to care. Like every parent with young children ever, taking care of Lilly leaves me with little left for much else.

Fighting with Ian is no fun anyway, and it's not because he's so good at persuasion because he's a lawyer. In their regular lives, lawyers are no more convincing than anyone else. There are no loopholes to exploit in real life, or maybe there are too many, I'm not sure anymore. All I know is that I've never wanted to convince anyone of anything. People don't want to be convinced. They want to be right. It is no fun arguing with Ian because there is no way to crack him open. He doesn't cry or get angry. He doesn't throw things or storm out of the house. He won't call you names. He won't acknowledge he's in the wrong, and on those rare occasions where he does, he's one of those who say sorry but never change—even if they mean it, especially if they mean it. My mind goes searching, as it has since my youth, for a song. I chose "Girl" by Tori Amos for our first dance at our makeshift, talent-show wedding, officiated by a non-denominational, humanist, lesbian celebrant. "Girl" is nearly impossible to two-step to but we didn't care. We whispered to each other, "She's been everybody else's girl, maybe one day she'll be her own," and it felt like some kind of promise truer than our overly-wrought, well-crafted vows.

Sit in the chair and be good now; the front door clicks. My heart leapfrogs into my throat and in that long instant I almost decide it is a lost cause and not worth the effort, but the Portuguese mother in me won't let it go. My mother ruled our house with an iron fist. Though my father was the titular head of the house, she was the real power. She worked a fulltime job. She handled all the bills and managed all the finances. My father, on the other hand, was a silent man. He went to work and lived for his soccer team. He would get this look on his face, sometimes, like he was looking between dimensions and was pulled toward it, like cats sometimes do. If he caught me looking, he would smile and go back to listening to the game, assuring his daughter in his way that everything was ok. But I never bought it. That's a look like seeing the face of god and finding a countenance like ice or stone. Is that what I look like now? Is that the face I show my daughter—a look lost in that place beyond exhaustion?

"We need to talk," I say the moment his foot touches the living room, lit by the one feeble lamp I purposefully left on for effect. I feel every ridiculous bit of this moment and am so tired I just want to go straight to bed.

"I'm tired," Ian says, his limp brown hair untethered, his briefcase stylishly distressed in the way of professional people.

"You're always tired."

"Let's not do this, please. I've had a long day."

"Not as long as mine."

"Is this a competition?"

"If you want to make it one," I say.

"Giselle, what do you want?"

"I've told you before not to call me by that name."

"It's your real name."

"Just because my parents gave me a name doesn't make it real. Stop pretending you don't understand."

"So, when Lilly wants to be called Illy, or some stupid thing, you're going to be ok with that?"

"Yes, that's exactly what it means. If she wants to be called Dogshit, that is what I'll call her."

"That is ridiculous," he says, looking resigned to the fact of our argument.

"You're ridiculous."

"If you're going to insult me, I'm going to bed. I've heard it all before."

"What is wrong with you?"

"With me? Nothing. I'm not the one calling you names. I'm being perfectly reasonable."

"Shut down isn't the same as reasonable."

"I'm sorry if I don't make a scene over every little thing."

"That's some pretty misogynistic bullshit, baby. This is fed up. That's what this is. Sitting here like an idiot waiting for you."

"That's not my fault."

"Right, because that is what matters—whose fault it is."

"I just can't win with you."

"Who cares about that?"

"What do you want from me?"

"Is this how you imagined it would go?"

"Yes, actually. Everything in its place. Everyone doing their part."

This catches me by surprise and stops me dead. I honestly don't know what to say. For the first time in years I realize just how different we really are. If he is telling the truth—and I think he is—then we are fundamentally different people. I guess I always knew it but never actually considered what it might mean, not really. Maybe no one ever does.

"G, please, what do you want from me?"

"I want you to love me …"

"I do love you—"

"Like I love you."

"I do," he says firmly.

"But it's an easy thing to say. You never do anything."

"That's not fair."

"Name me one time. One time you did something for me because you love me and for no other reason." To his credit, he does try to come up with an example but fails. There is no precedent to draw on.

"Do you know how long it's been since we made love?"

"Here we go again. Is that what this is really about?"

"Isn't it important to you at all?"

"Is that all that matters? Sex?"

"No, but …"

"When are you going to grow up?"

"When am *I* going to grow up?"

"Yes, I have more important things to think about than sex."

"Forget it. Fuck you."

"Keep your voice down. You'll wake Lilly," he says to antagonize me.

"You don't make the rules here. I make the rules."

"Who pays for this house?"

"I do."

"No, you do not."

"I clean this house. I fix whatever is broken. I cook all the meals. I raise our child IN THIS HOUSE. I set up playdates and birthday parties, and I deal with her school and her therapists. When something needs to be done, I do it. Not you. None of that is free. What do you do?"

"I pay the bills."

"Making money doesn't mean you pay for shit."

"You don't know what it's like in the real world."

"My life isn't the real world? Here's what's real, Ian. I give my time, all my time, to our family. Where do you give yours?"

"What did you think was going to happen when you married a lawyer?"

"Bullshit. Don't give me that bullshit. That didn't work when my father said it to my mother and it isn't going to work here either."

"See what happens if I stop working."

"If you want to go old school, then you're still not holding down your end because one of your jobs is to fuck me and you can't even do that."

"This is so stupid," he says.

"You know what. Forget it. Go to sleep. It's all you're good for."

"I plan to."

"And don't be surprised if I find another bed to crawl into." I hadn't intended to say that because I love his self-doubt, his fragile moral compass and deep sense of unworthiness, but he went too far. When he picked his job over Lilly, he went too far. There is no way I can take it back now, and some part of me doesn't want to. I've thought it often enough. Now I've said it. I've named it out loud.

"Go ahead. I don't really care," he says coldly. He drifts into the bedroom and it looks like it's over but then he surprises me by coming back out. "And I'll do you one better, you can have the bed. I'll sleep in the office from now on. There, now we good? Is that what you wanted? Now you can bring whomever you want. Just do it when I'm not home."

"You're never home, anyway."

"Then it should be really easy."

I stare at his back because he's already walking away, a reverse of our first meeting. The fight goes out of me. I never imagined he'd say those words.

"Do you mean it?" I'm not sad, not angry anymore. "Is that what you want?" He doesn't answer. "Ian, is it?"

"Do what you … need," he says from the other room and it sounds sad.

"You're what I need, god damn it."

"Please, just let me sleep."

"Ian."

"I'm sorry."

"You're sorry because you didn't mean it or because you did?"

"I'm sorry."

"Ian! Ian!"

And then he's gone. Before his shoes hit the floor, he is asleep:

> *And I'm callin' my baby*
> *Callin' my baby*
> *Callin' my baby*
> *Callin' everybody else's girl.*

I do not give you this song. I will give you your love back since it twins with mine, twines for mine, but I do not give you this song. I take back its shackles of syntax, its screws of punctuation, its bars of notes because I can no longer bind you to me. How do we fall? Is it, like this? Like a shadow to crawl in? Or is it, like this? Like winter's fallen cherry tree?

EM DASH

15

Twenty-six sightings of Chicago's infamous Flying Humanoid this winter. A new record. This is front page news? Riding the bus with all my roller derby gear is not fun under normal circumstances but with the rain slowing everything down, it's nothing short of a trial of character. I cannot be late for this bout because it is against our archrivals—the Windy City Rollers. A nasty fog kicks up by the time I reach my stop, so I can see only the barest outline of the rink and only because its floodlights bravely hold off the terrible whiteout. Strange things happen in mists like this. My best friend says she hears babies crying. Some people hear voices or singing, sad like the sad songs my mother played Sunday mornings as we readied for Portuguese Mass. Portuguese mariners saw rocks in every dark shadow and white crest, heard in the ticking silence sad longing songs from their lovers back in Lisbon, songs so tempting they had to lash themselves to the masts of their barques so they wouldn't throw themselves overboard. My fisherman's blood tells me it is dangerous to linger too long in the mist. As I rush to the rink with skates over my shoulder, I hear what sounds like my name from behind me.

"Emily."

There it is again. Something moves, something dark and lumbering, limping to a standstill. Before whatever it is breaks from cover, my full name rings out a third time, clear and distinct now—a name I do not use and barely recognize. And then it emerges, face paled by rain and eyes ready and hungry for wild work. I take half a step back as if giving myself time to recognize the form, not a trick of smoke but nearly as dangerous.

"What are you doing here?"

"Is that the first thing you say to me?"

"Ok. What the fuck are you doing here?" It breathes and I can measure the depth of its hot breath in spurts and waves. "I don't have time for this right now."

"You don't answer your phone," it says, lips unmoving.

"I know because I blocked you."

"You don't return my emails."

"That's what 'I blocked you' means."

"You're hurting me," says the creature who is also my father. When I don't answer, it changes tactics: "I was sick, you know. I almost died."

"Dad, I don't give a shit. That has nothing to do with me."

"You don't care if I die?"

"No," I say, but there is a slight catch and he hears it.

I must have summoned him, like some ancient demon winging the dark toward the bright sound of my voice. Some part of me must have wanted him to see me skate; some part of me must have wanted him to see the damage I can do or the damage I can take; some very secret part of me reached out to him and convinced him to come looking for his wayward daughter. Twenty-six sightings. A new record.

I came to roller derby late in life and was surprised to find a great gift for endurance. For some reason I can keep going

when others give up. I am not the fastest, nor the most skilled;
I'm certainly not the strongest, but I can keep going and going
like that stupid battery bunny, which should have earned me
the name, Energizer Betty, but the name was already taken. I go
down over and over again, but I always get back up. We derby
girls have a saying, "Go down seven, get up eight." We like the
bruises, the dings, the chipped teeth—even the track rash, the
hellacious and artful friction burns we get from sliding at high
speeds on parts of our bodies never meant for sliding on. Track
rash burns like rope, like Damascus whose distinction is found
in the watery, pattern forge welds of iron and steel. The quality
is in the fire—too much and it shatters, too little and its soft
belly will cut but once and then not so well. There is fire at the
center of most things, though it has learned to hide its face
under so many clever masks. It burns; it clears the underbrush
and makes all that is new run glad in its runnels—like our skate
wheels blazing a trail on the flats of the track.

He stands out of the rain in a bus shelter, assuming the guise
of sad old man. He is so good at this, though he is neither sad nor
old. A broken bottle rests at his feet and the Plexiglas is deeply
etched with warring tags. Tagging puts me in the mind of personal
failure and urban decay. Nothing to see but the often-incom-
prehensible moniker of some lost soul. Just a name on the wall,
unreadable, a grave stone worn from too many rains. It insists
upon itself and yet has nothing to insist on like my father, like
a mass hallucination, like this winter's record number of sightings of the Winged Humanoid—Chicago's legendary, six-foot
creature with red eyes who menaces the coast of Lake Michigan.

"We haven't told anyone, you know" the Winged Monster hisses seductively. "You can come back and it'll be like
nothing happened."

"Like when I was ten?"

"I don't know what you mean," it clicks, jerking a folded wing apoplectically.

When I was a child, I was really anxious, so anxious I went to the bathroom every twenty minutes. My parents pretended not to notice. The other kids hated me. My parents didn't care. Some little dickhead who lived on my street wrote, "Emily is a nerd" in giant chalk letters right in front of my house. When I told my father, he made me feel like it was my fault. When that same kid tried to steal my bike, I punched him in the throat and then he told his parents and I got in trouble. My parents didn't want to hear it. At school, I cried every single day. It's all good, they thought. Nothing to see here. Go about your business. They are Portuguese, see, but unlike most of my friends' parents, they aren't immigrants. They were raised in the U.S. Both sets of grandparents came over from the Azores before my parents were born. You would think this would be an advantage, but it wasn't. They didn't fit. On the one hand, they were still very much a part of the old world of the Azores, continuing the cultural traditions, speaking the language. On the other hand, they wanted to pass for locals. They had college educations, though they didn't do anything with them, deciding to work in the mills rather than risk failure elsewhere. They lived in perpetual contradiction as the two cultures tore them apart. And then they had a daughter like me, who was too American to be Portuguese, too Portuguese to be American, and too weird and strange to be much good for anything.

I honestly don't know when it started. One day I simply became aware I was doing something, but by this point I wasn't stupid enough to tell my parents about it or anyone else. It wasn't a decision I made. I am not even sure where the idea came from. I guess I must have been depressed, but in the 80's that was like saying you were abducted by aliens. In fact, I probably would have gotten a better sort of attention had I claimed alien abduction. Everyone likes a good probing now and then. Aliens were all the rage then as they are now satisfying as they do the basic human desire for something to kill with impunity, something to unite us in the solidarity of easy, clear, and simple hatred. Robots serve the same purpose. Monsters, not so much. Monsters have evolved. They are no longer the natural enemies of humanity; they have become the misunderstood victims of man's uglier impulses: Caliban, Frankenstein's Monster, Count Dracula, the Wolf Man—all creatures to be pitied and feared, to be sure, but not necessarily despised. I am not sure when that transition happened—when monsters, like fathers, became too close for comfort. Maybe it was always this way.

I honestly don't know when I started suffocating myself, but I had been doing it for a long time. When I did it, everything got quiet for a while. Maybe that night I only got up once or twice to go to the bathroom instead of every twenty minutes. It worked. That was all I knew and it was all that mattered. One night, without really thinking about it too much, I tried to hang myself, but I failed. That was it. Simple, honest, true. When I came to, no one was home. No one found me. At first, I woke to a feeling of profound wellbeing, soft and beautiful, as if I had had the first real sleep of my life. But then I remembered, I wasn't dead. Simply alive. I wasn't dead, and then I started to cry. I went to the emergency room because I didn't know what else to do. I was scared and I wasn't, and I couldn't be sure which was worse. All I knew was that I couldn't unknow what I knew and that life was long—so, so long. They called my parents because I was a minor and they came to pick me up red-faced and furious, so I refused to go home with them. I told the nurses I'd do it again if they made me go home with them, so I got to spend a couple weeks on a psych ward. It was perfectly boring. Perfectly, gloriously boring until my father came to visit. When I saw him, he said, "Can we be done playing this game, now? You're missing a lot of school," and for the first time I noticed his shadow did not match his body, that it reached clear across the room as if to envelop it or blow it away with a sweep of his raptor's wings. It slipped off a shoulder like a blanket chewed to fritters by a family dog or a cape at the end of a long night among the wolves. I refused to see him after that. When the hospital staff finally made me go home, my mother told all my relatives I had pneumonia.

We never spoke of it again. The secret was the beginning and end of our relationship. A secret can be an atrocity—it's always a surprise even when you know it's coming. And all you are left with is the feeling of regret that you just weren't prepared for it.

"Don't you think this has gone on long enough?" the Winged Humanoid clucked, his head an owl's swivel.

"You still think I'm coming back, don't you?"

"I'm sure of it."

"You and Mom have lost your minds."

"Your mother was waiting for you to call her on her birthday, you know."

I snort. He was always saying stuff like this. My father has very satisfactorily executed imitations of human behavior. Did he hope that if he pretended to be human long enough he would actually become one? Did my mother? Do I? How close is too close for comfort?

"We did our best."

"Then your best sucks."

"We did what we thought was right."

"I was never the daughter you wanted, and you never forgave me for that."

"That is not true. How were we supposed to know when you were throwing a tantrum and when …"

"Say it. Say the words. When I was trying to kill myself."

"We didn't know."

"Oh god. You're circling back to stupid again?"

"I am stupid. I am."

"That won't save you. This shit doesn't work on me anymore."

"What do you want?" he asked and a talon shot out like a blade, like he wanted to shred me to strips of meat.

"I don't want anything from you."

"Please …"

"Please, nothing. I don't want to see you again, and that is it."

"Emily."

I turn to leave. "Emily!" The last thing I want to do is play derby now, but if I don't get away from him, I know he is going to keep circling, riding the thermals with his great leather wings until he wears me out. Even my endless gas tank fails. That's how he gets what he wants. He wears you down until you can't fight back. You go down and don't get back up, but I'm a derby girl now.

"You know, your mother said not to bother with you," he says, deepening the glow of those monster's eyes. "You were always spoiled."

"Don't you dare say that again!"

"I don't know where we went wrong, but I don't like the person you've become. You're not a nice person."

"You don't get to decide that. You don't decide anything here."

By now, a few other late skaters have gotten off the bus, women who understand what is owed and what isn't, who escaped the wilderness like I did but knew how it could still stalk you and drag you back beneath the soil. When they see me, they know something is not right and come to my rescue.

"Em, you ok?"

"I'm fine. He was just leaving."

"Take a walk, creep, before something bad happens to you," says all six feet, 180 pounds of Sylvia Wrath.

"Yeah, get the fuck out of here," echoes Pain Eyre.

"Who the fuck was that?"

"I don't know. Some loser," I say walking toward the rink, wondering what more could go wrong—not the best mindset to start a derby bout in. One must be careful with this sort of thing. "What else can go wrong?" is not rhetorical, it's a dare and someone or something is always listening. Twenty-six sightings of the Chicago Flying Humanoid this winter. A new record. Twenty-six. He must have been looking for me. Unclean wings fan out of my father's back and he shoots deep into the night sky, high above Lake Michigan and swoops back to shadow the cold lawns and forlorn streets of the small east coast town that reared me—alone and misunderstood as all monsters are. How does it end? Like this? Like the answer to a question? Like a question answered with another question? Or is it, like this? An incomplete phrase, an interruption ... a tumble into the suicide seats at top speed.

FROST HEAVES
EMMANUEL

16

Nights before I teach my Dev-Ed writing class are brutal.
My students know that I never miss class. I get sick so rarely,
but the only thing that's stopping me from inventing a fatal
disease for myself is the thought of having to deal with the
poor substitute teacher who walks into the minefield of this
class, which has been terrorized by one student all semester.
It only takes one; that is how delicate an ecosystem a classroom can be. In the student's defense, she can't help it. She's
schizophrenic, I think. It's not her fault, but I'm not trained to
handle situations like this and her classmates are bearing the
brunt of her constant distractions. I live in fear of being found
out, of being revealed—deathly afraid of being blamed for her
behavior, because, more importantly, I am hoping to land one
of the (increasingly-rare) full-time positions that have been
recently announced in the department, so I can't afford any
negative attention.

This institution is better than most about hiring from its
own adjunct pool; some places will not even consider you if
you've taught in their department—as if you have been tainted
forever by failure. The work may only be part time, but the
failure isn't. Failure is full time with no benefits. Two years ago,

I made it all the way to the final round, so I thought I might be next in line for a tenured position. I didn't get the job the first time due to lack of experience, or so they said, and the person they hired wasn't an internal candidate. It stands to reason they might hire internally this time around, so I bite down and come to every single class, but it's gotten so bad that I have to pop a few Xanax before class begins or I won't make it. If I liked to drink, I'd certainly have tried that too, but what's more cliché than a boozy writing professor, not that I have ever met one in real life, not in this market. Who can afford booze on this pay? On more than one occasion, I have found myself weeping in my office, and that's how you know things have gotten bad—an adult crying in his room because he doesn't want to go to school.

If this keeps up, I will soon look like my sweet grand-mother who raised seven children during Salazar's fascist Estado Novo in Portugal—bent, aged, haunted, defeated. I have no idea what I am going to do about this particular stu-dent's grade. I knew it was going to be a problem from the moment she handed in her first, nearly-incomprehensible essay. A practical person would just give her the C and be done with it. Too much was on the line for silly ideals. No one cares. It won't change her life. She isn't going to land some sen-sitive job because she got a passing grade in my basic writing class. She will not be operating on any patients or building a bridge or designing rockets. A person of integrity, on the other hand, would give the student the failing grade she earned and deal with the consequences because being right has to matter at some point, even in situations such as these—and I am definitely in the right. Of course, assholes say the exact same thing. There are so many people who are absolutely assured of their rightness, the world may not be able to sustain even one more of that kind.

I am sad to say I dream often of telling her off, of flunking her and dismissing her from my life with a final, wordless gesture. Or if forced to pass her—which happens more often than you think—I imagine saying that the passing grade came from the Dean and not from me, like I did once to a student who complained when I was a grad TA and far more uncompromising. I'm not someone who wishes to be young again. I wouldn't be a teenager for all the world, or even in my 20s, but I do miss being outrageously uncompromising; I miss the confidence that comes from too-limited a perspective, but it's not something an adult can afford to indulge too much in. More than anything, I want it to be over. I want her out of my life. There is nothing I can do for her and so much she can do to me.

Gomez enters the room. "Listen to this," he says, "'One park ranger is dead and three more are injured in … a recent firefight with rebels in the Democratic Republic of Congo. The death marks the first ranger killed since January in Virunga National Park, which is home to famed mountain gorillas and has lost 140 rangers to violence in the past few years.'"

"That's horrible."

He continues reading: "'Virunga … is one of the most contested zones on Earth and has been at the center of the DRC's civil wars for decades. The ongoing conflict decimated the mountain gorilla population … But thanks to its committed force of rangers Virunga is undergoing a resurgence. The mountain gorilla population has increased to 880.' Is that where *Gorillas in the Mist* took place?"

"No, that was in Rwanda, but it's on the other side of the Virunga Mountains."

"Look at you, with the facts."

"She was murdered, you know."

"Who?"

"Dian Fosse," I say.

"Really?"

"Machete to the skull."

"Jeez. My ignorance depresses me. All I know about Africa is Egyptian gods, *The Lion King*, Shaka Zulu, and Nelson Mandela."

"That's because those are all movies."

"Oh, and *The Ghost and the Darkness*."

"The Val Kilmer movie?"

"Yup."

"You and your Val Kilmer movies. What was the Western you liked so much? *Tombstone*?"

"Love that movie. I can't help it if Val and I have synchronicity."

"Ugh, I hate that word."

"Right? Like one of those horrible business catchwords that don't mean anything but sound fancy."

"Exactly, like *buy-in*," I say.

"And *scalable*."

"Gross."

"Poor things ended up in the Field Museum, you know," says Gomez.

"Who?"

"The Ghost and The Darkness, the real man-eating lions of Tsavo."

"Didn't realize it was based on a real event."

"Yes, it is. They're stuffed, poor things."

"What an undignified way to go."

"Exactly. Those two lions singlehandedly took on the British Empire and look what happens to them? They end up a couple of stuffies in a glass box," says Gomez, warming to his subject.

"America."

"America."

"That's an interesting way to look at it."

"How else would you look at it? They stalled the building of a major railway and killed 30 people and a mattress."

"A mattress?"

"One of the lions attacked a worker in a tent, got confused or something and carried off his mattress instead."

"So much for the killer instincts of apex predators," I say.

"Who are we to question evolution's sharp razor? Can you imagine if your job was lion hunter? I mean, what's it like to wake up in the morning, brush your teeth, look in the mirror and think, 'I'm a fucking lion hunter!'"

"Pretty terrible, I'd hope. Killing off those amazing cats."

"Yes, yes, but let's say you're not like one of those dick-head, rich-boy trophy hunters. I mean, fuck those guys, but you're like a hunter, a real hunter—for necessity or what have you. That's got to be a pretty singular vocation. How does one get there?"

"No clue … Do you think there is still such a thing as a vocation?"

"I'd love to say yes, but I'm not so sure."

I tell Gomez about Sheila Siddle and her husband—a British couple with no formal training or interest in primates—who ended up establishing a chimp sanctuary in Zambia. I can barely imagine living in a world where that sort of thing could still happen, where you'd be in your home going about your life and then suddenly a stranger shows up with a severely hurt chimp and before you know it a mission has found you. Every idea of who or what you were or were going to be gets thrown out overnight. One second you are a cattle rancher, then suddenly you're building a five-mile enclosure on your own dime to house a slowly growing family of chimps. I'd give anything for that kind of inevitability and so would many people, I imagine.

I thought teaching was my mission, but unlike the Siddles, no one has come to my door in the middle of the night with a baby chimp bundled in their arms. In fact, the harder I try to land it, the less inevitable it seems. There is only so long one can knock on a door before it becomes ridiculous to be standing there in the rain and cold with the neighbors watching behind the blinds shaking their heads piteously. I don't want to have the wrong dreams. I don't want to die without ever having lived, or rather, die thinking I am a failure when I am—or could have been—happy.

"I need to tell you something."

"That sounds ominous," says Gomez.

"What do you think about me not teaching anymore?"

"Oh. Uh, I don't know. What's up?"

"If I was going to get a full-time job, it would have happened by now, don't you think?"

"Not necessarily."

"I mean, at what point is this just an act of self-mutilation?"

"I don't know, *Cara Mia*. Not sure there is a point on the graph that indicates that."

Gomez knows me so well. He knows I've been running the numbers all this time, and every year that passes the conclusion becomes clearer and clearer. My probability matrix tells me failure is imminent; luck will not be on my side; the equation will not balance out over time. Acting against this seemingly obvious logic is doing more damage than the disappointment itself. I cannot survive in an atmosphere of illogic, in the despair of unrelenting and meaningless hopefulness. I cannot simply repeat the same experiment without changing the parameters and hope for a different conclusion. But to fail now is to fail not just myself, not just Gomez, but all the students I promised (by the sheer fact of teaching them) a better future, and, also, my family. The enormous weight of it is unendurable.

Gomez's parents, like mine, had come to this country to find better opportunities for their children. The shit of it was that they had succeeded—sort of. We should be on a poster for the American Dream—a proof that though it doesn't always happen, it happens enough to sustain the idea in the face of obvious contradiction. The lottery works on the same dubious principal. We had been the first in our families to graduate high school and go to college. And in deciding to teach at community colleges instead of universities, we had the chance to help mold people who would otherwise go unnoticed. What they didn't tell us was that the distance between theory and practice wore at you unceasingly. More than anything, we hated being the gate keepers. We didn't want to shut the door in the faces of people who've had enough of that already. And we certainly didn't want to do it at these prices. Who could live off part-time pay? Easy answer: no one. They didn't tell us about this when we were in graduate school. They didn't even seem aware.

"You're still young. You never know when the long odds will finally come out in your favor," says Gomez giving me the old party line he no longer really believes.

"The odds are far too long. I'm tired. I want to buy a house and go on vacations and have a car. Do you miss it?"

"Teaching? Yes. Grading, no. Being a second-class citizen, not even a little bit. But I miss the idea of it still sometimes. I miss who I wanted to be."

"Yes, exactly."

"I went to grad school and all I got was this lousy diploma. Sadly, I will never get to write my magnum opus, *I Drank What? Val Kilmer and the Making of American Culture, 1980-2000.*

"Truly a great loss to scholarship."

"I think so. *Real Genius* should have set the standard for smart kids in America, not that piece of shit *Revenge of the Nerds. Real Genius* is about taking on the man, thwarting his war fantasies with science and a giant, god-sized Jiffy Pop. *Revenge of the Nerds* is just *Animal House* but with taped glasses and pocket protectors—reductive, misogynistic, and rapey. It's repulsive." Gomez looked up to see that I was not listening. "What's the plan?"

"No clue. Want to adopt a baby?"

"You're kidding, right?" he says sounding concerned.

"Yes, I am totally kidding."

"Don't scare me like that. I'll support whatever you want to do, you know that. You could always try something else and go back to teaching if it doesn't work out. Who knows, maybe other employment experience will make you more marketable. It couldn't hurt at this point."

"Maybe."

"Let's see if you get the job this time around before we do anything too rash."

EM
DASH

17

"He almost died right there."

"That's really scary, Em," says Gilga. "Why do you do this stuff? First it was kickboxing, then roller derby, now fencing?"

"Well, it was a freak thing. It was a complete clusterfuck of bad luck."

"It worries me."

"It's not like it happens all the time."

The first Friday of every month we have a fight night at our gym where we can practice our sword techniques in live sparring. It is relatively safe. As far as I know, there had never been a serious injury at this school, nothing scarier than some bruises, a twisted ankle or two, a hyperextended elbow here and there. But you know how these things go—it's always a black swan moment. The school has very strict safety regulations: all safety equipment must be checked before sparring, only three bouts may take the floor at a time, every bout must be observed by a high-ranking student, new students must spar with instructors, and a first aid kit must be within easy reach of each list. You trick yourself into believing that since nothing bad has happened before it can't happen now, but that is not how the world really works.

I found fencing because I needed something physical to do. I have kind of lost my taste for derby. I am still playing, but, to be honest, I am not really into it, anymore. I'm not sure why. I've begun missing practices and skipping bouts. My coaches are not very happy with me, nor are my teammates. It's no fun playing on a team when everyone is disappointed in you. I know this will likely be my last season, but I still need the release. One day, I saw a Facebook ad for a school that teaches Historical European Martial Arts. It is the actual stuff a gentleman of the Renaissance would have used to guard his fragile honor, which, it turns out, was constantly under attack. When I saw the ad, I was already glove slapping people all over the city for even the slightest of perceived insults, even though I was pretty sure that was not going to be part of the curriculum, though the long gloves, I was happy to find, would be. I'm pretty sure every person who dreams of playing with rapiers has the glove fantasy. Someone on the Greenline sitting in a handicapped seat who shouldn't be—slap! Someone blaring their terrible music on the 72 North Ave bus—double slap. Anyone mansplaining in my vicinity at any time and I slap them to within an inch of their life. I was smart enough to keep this fantasy to myself.

I went to three rapier classes and knew this sport was for me. I spent hundreds of dollars on gear immediately—not that I should have spent that kind of money. That pretty much cleared me out, but it was worth it. Who needed food, who needed a place to sleep when you could wield steel? I bought a jacket, some leather gloves, a gorget, and, of course, my very own rapier. It's quite different from sport or Olympic fencing. Sport fencing uses very small and light foils, which are modelled on the eighteenth-century court or small sword, so-called because they were easier to wear at court than the far more unwieldy rapier. Imagine the schtick of a gentleman bowing and lifting the skirts of some powdered and bewigged lady standing several feet behind him. The small sword did develop from the Renaissance rapier and is, therefore, a direct descendent of the sword I am learning to use, but they are very different in terms of technique. The rapier is much longer, much heavier, and uses the large and elaborate hilt as an integral part of defense and counterattack. The small sword is much shorter, has a minimal guard, and relies primarily on speed. Rapier blades are flat and have a sharp edge that can cut, though cutting is not the primary attack of a rapier. The small sword may or may not have a cutting edge since it lacks the heft for cutting. When I look up, I can tell I am boring poor Gilga to death with my Rapier 101 lesson, but I can't stop myself and she's kind enough to pretend to be interested. Swords are easy to geek over.

On the fight night I was telling Gilga about, two of the more senior students were sparring pretty hard. They both had years of experience so this was no surprise, nor was it looked down upon. If a novice was going that hard, she would certainly get a stern talking to, but it is the privilege of study to be allowed to get closer to full strength. They're not reenactors and this isn't stage combat. They're trying to get as close as possible to the experience of actual historical fencing by studying the manuscripts of Fabris, Capo Ferro, Silver, Agrippa, and others, and putting their techniques to the test. During one of the exchanges, one of the students came in from a low angle with a quick thrust and the blade somehow found a gap in the bib of his helmet. It missed—through sheer bad luck—the gorget, which provides secondary protection to the throat, and went into the student's neck. The sword should have had a rubber blunt on the point, but it must have been knocked-off during the exchange, which can happen. I thought I was about to watch someone die right before my eyes and from a sword wound, no less. Thankfully, they managed to stabilize him long enough for the paramedics to arrive. The sword missed his carotid artery by mere inches. It was scary, and I felt awful for the other guy who never intended to hurt his fencing partner. Maybe he wished in that moment that their places were reversed—and I understood that idea very well.

"And why do you do this?"

"It's fun."

"Sounds it."

"Don't be sarcastic. This is probably way safer than derby or kickboxing or taking a shower, for that matter."

"But what purpose does it serve?" asks Gilga, a little exasperated.

"Manny would say probably zombies."

"Right? Why is everything zombies now?"

"Zombies don't carry guns," I say in an overly serious manner, just like Manny would, imitating the voice he always used when he went into teacher mode. "Democrats should really work on getting that ever-important zombie vote if they're going to make any headway on this gun issue. I keep saying it, but do they listen? No." We laugh, missing our friend's weird sense of humor suddenly. He's been on my mind a lot lately, ever since I saw him at the derby bout.

"Yes, he would have said something like that, I am sure. Do you ever speak to him?" Gilga asks knowing the answer.

I have not spoken to him since the band broke up twenty years ago. I'm not even sure why, anymore. I feel bad for running out on him and on everyone else. At the same time, I am equally afraid of overestimating my importance. I mean, it was high school. What seems the size of the universe turns out to be nothing but a nutshell. Isn't that what Hamlet said? Nutshell? Peanut shell? I don't know. There's nothing more humiliating than finding out that the people you consider pivotal in your life don't feel the same way about you. Like this guy who used to follow the band around back in the day; apparently, I kissed him one night after a gig and twenty years later he looks me up on Facebook to tell me I was one of the great loves of his life. I didn't even remember him. We had exactly one make-out session, apparently, but that's how things get distorted over time as we turn up the volume on the parts we like and turn down others—covering them with distortion or chorus or reverb—to get our pasts to sound studio perfect. And so much time has gone by, I fear that I too may have remastered things a bit too much. I thought it was better to just leave it alone—until I saw him at the derby bout. I was so shocked I didn't know what to do and the jam was still on so I skated away. That was one hell of a shit night. First, my father, then Manny.

"I never did ask you, but why the disappearing act?"

"I don't know. Scared, I guess."

"Of touring?"

"Yes and no. Scared of disappointing everyone, which, of course, I made sure to do by leaving. I don't know." How could I explain to her that I could not bear to see the looks on their faces, especially Manny's, the look of profound disappointment that marred my parents' faces since the day I was born. How they looked at me like punishment. How they cursed the universe because I wasn't the daughter they wanted. Other children didn't cry all the time. Other children didn't have to stop every twenty minutes to go to the bathroom. Other children didn't end up in mental hospitals. So I ran for it and never looked back. Then I heard about Lilly. And suddenly I didn't want to run anymore. I needed to be there for this child, this child who was so much like me.

"Why didn't you guys just go on without me?"

"We tried. Manny switched to bass and we played a few gigs, but it was never the same. It felt all wrong. Manny slowly lost all interest and was only doing it out of loyalty to me. And then Kid's parents said that under no circumstances was he allowed to go on tour. That's not how they said it, of course. They said something more like, "You crazy? No, and that's it! Corisco, rapaz.""

"That sounds about right," I laugh sadly.

"So, we were back to square one, searching for drummers again, and then everyone seemed to give up. We didn't have a meeting or even talk about it. We just stopped playing. Manny got more and more into his new boyfriend, and Ash packed it up and went to California never to be heard from again. And, well, here we are."

"Give or take a few years."

"Yeah, give or take."

"I'm really sorry."

"No need to be sorry. It wasn't your fault."

"Yes, it was. We should have gone. I fucked it up."

"Don't know. I've got a wall around that time. When I think about that girl, the one with the singular focus, it breaks my heart, not that the band failed but that it was so easy to just move on, blame others, shrug my shoulders. I guess I was hoping for it to stick, for a wound to open, for despair. It didn't really come. Maybe it wasn't so special," says Gilga.

"It was. You did what you had to do to move forward. It was special, more special than I knew."

Gilga shrugs almost involuntarily, like she wants me to convince her but only a little bit. Lilly comes in and interrupts. She's six and wants to know which three Pokémon I would choose to take into battle. Gilga gives me a look that says she answers this question and others like it a hundred times a day. I don't really know any Pokémon, so I ask her to list a few and I'll pick from the list. She goes on for a good ten minutes demonstrating her encyclopedic knowledge of their powers, their types, their strengths and weaknesses. She brings in a book with so many cramped cross-referenced charts and numbers, it looks like one of Manny's probability matrices. Manny is in the air today, I guess. Ultimately, I choose Charmander. She says she likes fire types too but that electric types are the best. Then she runs off into the living room to watch the rest of her show, bouncing off the furniture like one of her Beyblades, and running a nonstop stream of commentary like I've seen her do many times.

Watching TV for Lilly is not a passive sport. Nothing is. She acts out what she sees and then when the moment is right, veers off on her own narrative that usually includes lots of explosions and attacks and counterattacks. I remember Gilga used to do this when she was her daughter's age; that's how long we've known each other. Everything was on a mythic scale for Gilga. It was *The Odyssey*; it was *The Aeneid, The Lusiads, The Epic of Gilgamesh*. It was *ThunderCats* and *He-Man*. Hence the name, The Great Gilgamesh. Gilga had given names, powers, backstories, and intrigues to all her toys, very much like Lilly's Pokémon. Gilga's mother initially attempted to make her play with other toys, but Gilga would have none of it and her mother was just too tired from working all day and then running the house to bother about something so inconsequential. Portuguese parents don't understand the American obsession with their children, not that they love them any less or any worse. They expect that you act the part of well-behaved child in public, but the rest of the time you are on your own. The worst thing that could be said for a child was that she was a malcriada—a brat. Portuguese parents have no interest in entertaining you, nor do they worry too much about how much TV you watch or how many snacks you eat. We didn't take naps during the day. We didn't do playdates. We didn't go to nursery school. They didn't read to us. Some of us turned out ok and some of us didn't, and that was just the way of things.

When I turned from watching Lilly run away, her child-energy too much for the walls of this house to contain, Gilga was wiping away tears.

"What's the matter? Hey, are you ok?"

Gilga did that smile-cry thing we all do when we're caught off guard and don't know if we're going to pretend everything is cool or if we're going to tell the truth.

"What is it?"

She shook her head but could not get any words out.

"Gilga. What's wrong?"

"It's Ian. We're getting a divorce."

FROST HEAVES
EMMANUEL

18

I want to say I failed that student. I want to say she forgave my failure. I want to say it all worked out for the best, that I landed the job, beating the odds and thwarting my loser matrix. I never did see her again, and I don't know if she's still out there somewhere torturing another class and another teacher. When I applied for the job this year, I didn't even get called for an interview after having made it to the final two candidates a couple years earlier. What could have changed so much in two years? If anything, I am better now than I was then. When I cornered the department chair to ask what I could improve for the next time—the politic way of asking, "Why the fuck didn't I get the job?"—she said I needed to make sure my student evaluations were better. And then I knew exactly what had happened—the student had written me a lousy evaluation. Or if it wasn't her, it was some other student (or students) who had been at her mercy for an entire semester. Or it might have been both. Or, it might not have been any of those things. Maybe I'm just a lousy teacher.

After 15 years, you can't still be the new jammer. I have been sent to my knees enough times now to know I don't belong on the line with the starred panty. Time to hang up the skates; time to put away the booty shorts, the fishnets, and the ghoulish face paint. Time to leave the work to others. Time to stash the dry erase markers and the PowerPoints. Oh, my Em. I know you saw me; you looked into my eyes. You saw me. How does one leave? How does one break from the script?

CHICAGO 2016

To: FrostheavesManny4646@gmail.com

From: GomezA@hotmail.com

Cara Mia,

I cannot believe we are apart. I don't know where you are right now. You left only a short time ago, but I am unable to do a damn thing today. I just never thought we'd be doing this at this point in our lives. And now you've run off to California without me. When you said, "Maybe, we're better apart," I think you were joking or at least it started as a joke, but the more I think about it the more frightened I become. Is there more to this than I am aware? Is there more to this than you are aware?

When I left academia, my biggest fear was that we wouldn't have anything in common anymore. This part of the narrative is as old as our relationship. It is the oldest river-cut stones of our relationship, or if not the stones at least the mortar in the walls we made. I know you said this year would be "an experiment," but I know better than to underestimate your experiments and the epiphanies they can bring. We both know epiphanies are ruthless and without mercy. They destroy as easily as they unfetter. I think of poor Mrs. Mallard in "Story of an Hour," how the liberation of one hour led to her immediate and tragic death.

What enchanted moments will I miss, darling? What rough men will you see glinting in the desert sun; what rare women will you meet in the glades on horseback while I slog about my boring days? I've lost an eye. You are my left eye, or my right. The world will lack luster and depth as it batters relentlessly at my blind spot. I am so proud of you, but just make sure to come back to me, ok? I am there with you. How does my heart break? Is it, like this? Like the joy that kills?

Always,
Gomez

EM DASH

20

I kept waiting for the cops to show up. For weeks now, I've been jumping every time my phone rings and grow rigid and tense whenever a police cruiser passes me. I promise myself that if I don't get arrested, I'll never do something so stupid again—and I mean it. But my determination, like most determinations, only enjoys a touch of wisdom, just a wisp, and it doesn't take long for my stupidity to return, and I very quickly desire to duel again. Then the Canadians go and decriminalize challenging people to duels. To be clear, they didn't make duels legal again, which is how the clickbait made it sound, just the act of challenging people to duels, but it still feels like the universe is urging me on, daring me to test my steel once again.

It was like my first kickboxing match. Before the fight, I was really scared, a fear so utterly primitive I vowed I would never do it again. Backstage, warming up, walking to the ring, the words repeated on an endless loop: "I will never do this again." I used it, took power from it, made those words steady my legs, which seconds before were spongy and ready to collapse: "I will never do this again." I made the repetitions force my legs forward towards my opponent rather than in the opposite direction, which is what my brain was commanding me to do: "I will never do this again." But from the second the first kick was thrown, from the moment the first punch landed solidly on my forehead, all was forgotten. Not only did the loop stop, the words were cast down into the dirt, cast aside like a belief you thought was holding up the universe's pants but now seemed to have no actual function. In fact, it felt downright silly—a child's way of thinking.

In my corner between the first and second round, my former-champion, tough-as-nails Mexican boxing coach was trying to give me advice on how to beat this girl and I heard none of it. All I remember saying was, "I can't wait to do this again." And he looked at me sternly and said, "Can we finish this one first?" Sadly, I never did fight again, but it wasn't from lack of trying. Three fighters backed out of my next fight, then my coach left the gym over some bull I never got the details to, and the new coach (who had beaten an aged and washed-up Mike Tyson) didn't give a crap about me for some inexplicable reason. I lost momentum and before I could find a new gym and a new coach, derby came and found me. I went from the ring to the rink. But derby too has had its day and now I play with swords.

The problem is that fencing in the modern world is mostly pretend—a game. The techniques are real enough, but the situation, obviously, is not. In kickboxing, by contrast, you're really punching and kicking someone, and they are really punching and kicking you back—even in sparring. In derby, you are cruising at terrific speeds on tiny wheels while getting smashed by shoulders and hips, learning about the relationship between force, mass, and acceleration in a way you never did in physics class. You learn how a floor can be a threat, how a hip can menace, how a shoulder can make you wince. But in fencing, there is no sharp edge, no point, and being touched with a practice blade has no consequence, leaves a bruise far less baroque than the ones I sustained on the track. It isn't anything like being stabbed by a real weapon. I admit I was already starting to lose interest in fencing when the fateful accident occurred that fight night, which is really messed up. I could make it real, I realized. What was wrong with me? It was not the lesson I was supposed to learn but I learned it none-theless. I could make it real if I had the courage and if I could find other people stupid enough to do it with me. And so not a month after the first time in the basement, I found myself on Craigslist again trying to find another opponent. And I found someone just as easily as the first time. It is obvious there are more idiots out there like me than I had initially thought. The idea is calming in its way. It turns out that being among idiots is so much better than feeling like the only idiot.

Back in the basement, I know right away that this woman is better than me—way better. She knows it too and it is clear in the fearless and bored way she's handling me. When I lunge sloppily and am wide open, she holds back. Then she passes forward so quickly I don't even see it, but instead of running me through, she breaks measure. It's like she's waiting for me to realize something, so I tell her to stop playing around and do something. I don't think this is what she is expecting. She simply nods and in the next pass sticks the point of her rapier right into my helmet, forcing my head back in that embar-rassing way that fencers and boxers know all too well, when something gets through your guard that shouldn't have and you are stunned by the mere fact of it. In kickboxing, a supe-rior fighter will literally wipe their foot on your face as the ultimate insult. The steel helmet, however, protects me from having a blade stuck dead in my brain pan. I should be dead, struck down like a shot, but I don't have a scratch on me.

"You lose," she says. "Stop this nonsense before you get hurt or worse," and she grabs her gear and walks out without looking back with a haughty and easy style I will never master. She could have killed me with little effort, but she didn't. Losing doesn't bother me. I'd lost my kickboxing match and that didn't even slow me down. I'd lost derby bouts before. Losing is no big deal once you realize no one cares about losses, only wins. I lost the fencing match, it's true; I lost the game but not the duel because in the end there was no duel. She'd robbed me of the duel or rather, to be fair, I'd robbed myself by wearing too much protective gear. I am not really dueling. This is dishonest. It has no meaning like this and I am ashamed.

FROST HEAVES EMMANUEL 21

Near my giant duplex—so big it could fit our entire apartment in Chicago several times over—is a grove of eucalyptus trees, well, "grove," I don't know. What makes a grove? There are two rows of trees lining a small section of bike path about a block long. Every time I walk the path, I think of koalas and how they must smell. Merced is a land of smells: trains streaming by in the night making the valley reek of garlic and onions from nearby Gilroy and Turlock, the ever-present hint of pesticides failing miserably to combat the nearly-biblical level plague of insects. Never have I seen a land of such extremes. The Central Valley is America's cornucopia, where we get most of our almonds, artichokes, dates, figs, raisins, tangerines, kiwi, olives, pistachios, prunes, pomegranates, walnuts—says Wikipedia—but it is also a desert. Leave the confines of this small town and you hit giant plantations, not farms but huge swaths of land manned almost entirely by machines, a kind of empty *Matrix* efficiency at play. I think of Keanu Reeves. He's one of ours too—has a Portuguese grandmother, I think. These machines are supplemented by itinerant workers whose hidden encampments are something out of the long memories of nomadic peoples. Head south on Route 99 towards Fresno, however, and there is only arid land, something waiting to finally be rid of us, dotted here and there with a few unmarked factories belching out a stink so terrible it induces panic for miles. It is a place of bleached bones, where carrion birds can be seen circling for miles in a flat blue sky, a place where water is rare and precious.

When the snows of Yosemite melt and flood the little creeks hitherto dry and nearly as invisible as thin scars on fair skin, the land turns an astonishing green—made astonishing by its stark contrast to the pitiful yellow-brown of the summers like a crumbling of dog hair. Wild roses bloom in places you thought were nothing but brittle, sun-scorched dirt lots. Mists rise dense and baffling, confounding both the eyes and the ears, fog banks burly enough for time to lose its shape in and for words to bend unbidden and unwanted. I can see why early peoples feared the mists and what lurked therein. This is not the California the rest of the country fantasizes about when they say West Coast. This isn't the Golden Gate Bridge or the Pacific Ocean, not the suntans and muscles of Los Angeles, nor the bohemians of Venice Beach; it isn't surfing or Berkley, not hair metal and rich weirdos in the hills. It is definitely not Hollywood. It's cattle ranches, evangelical Christians, and the Hmong. It couldn't be more distant from the little east coast city I grew up in, or the college towns of Western Massachusetts, or the busy urban center of Chicago. This is an America I have only read about, an America I have very little direct knowledge of.

There isn't much to do in Merced. There are a handful of fast food joints, a Starbucks, a grocery store, and a "nicer" restaurant or two—and most of these are of recent provenance. Not much else to do here, but in the lack there is abundance of a different kind. People depend on each other here, not because of some false sense of small-town values but out of necessity. When the land threatens to bring you to dust, you must grow hearts filled with dirt in order to survive. How much dirt is in my heart? From the moment I arrived in California, Gomez has been bombarding me with emails. At first, it was reassuring for his voice to find me across the vast majority of this continent, but his persistence has begun to annoy me. I am tired and don't have the time to write as much as he would like. I'm teaching a full load, have committee work, and my tenure project to consider. The first year of a tenure contract is the most precarious. They can let you go for no reason, and I am determined not to give them one to be rid of me. I don't think another chance like this is going to come my way. This might be it for me, the datum that balances the math in my loser matrices, that counters all that lost time in Chicago, that gives sense to the shape I gave myself at 18. I got one chance and I'm not going to blow it. I won't go back to part-time teaching. When I run the numbers, they finally come out on my side, but there is too much at stake for me to feel any real comfort in these odds.

When the call finally came that I had landed the English position at the University of California, Merced, I cried. I cried for an hour in the shower, my hands shaking from relief, from the release of so many years disappointment. I had made up my mind that this would be my last attempt, and, to be honest, I almost didn't go through with it. That student left me in tatters. It was only some kind of perversity—some demon whispering in my ear, making bargains—that convinced me to try. I'd spent years developing my application materials. It took nothing to send them out ONE LAST TIME, I reasoned.

What was there to lose? Somewhere I must have realized that there is only one thing I haven't done all these years I have been trying to land a full-time job; I haven't done a national search. I have been trying, for obvious reasons, to land a job in the Chicagoland area, but I never considered applying to all open positions regardless of where they were. I was told by my professors that location mattered and that living somewhere you hated would negate any advantages a job would provide; however, I could no longer afford such niceties. And there was Gomez to think about as well.

I was so sure it would make no difference that I didn't even tell Gomez I was applying to other jobs. People who have trouble having children always say they finally managed to get pregnant after they had given up, so I did the same. It didn't make any logical sense, but what did I have to lose at this point but my self-respect? Maybe if the universe thought I truly didn't care anymore, it'd stop being such a bastard and let one slip through—and, unbelievably, one did. Or, maybe, I was afraid Gomez would try to convince me not to go for it—or was it the opposite? Would I really leave him for a job? Would I trade all that we'd built to satisfy this one desire—or was it a need? When I landed the campus visit, I told him I was going to visit Gilga in Massachusetts. I hated lying to Gomez. It might have been the first time I had ever deliberately kept anything from him, never mind deceived him, but since I wasn't going to get this job, anyway, what harm could it do? One day, we'd play Truth or Dare like we did that first time in my dorm room, and I'd admit that I had lied to him and we'd have such a laugh about it, about how foolish I had been to run off to rural California without telling him. He'd be surprised that after all these years there were still things he did not know about me, and he would love it. He would love that there was still a spot he hadn't touched.

I returned from Merced and told myself I didn't care about the job, that it was just good to know I was still competitive, so there was no reason to worry about it. And who wanted to live in the middle of nowhere? I'm a city boy. Merced was too small, even smaller and more nowhere than Somerset. I'd never be happy there. And then I actually forgot about it, which is amazing. We have such skill in fooling ourselves.

And then the call came.

When I told Gomez, he was stunned—a painful smile stuck to his face that was fooling no one. He was able to buy himself some time while I apologized profusely for keeping it from him. He put on an elaborate show of happiness, which must have cost him something, though some part of it was authentic. You see, there's something you need to know about Gomez. He's so proud that sometimes he does things that are harmful to himself because he'd rather hold on to that pride than lower himself in his own mind. But the real world is not soft enough for ideals.

In his foolish pride, he isn't considering all the angles. He isn't considering the fact that people do not know themselves as well as they claim. Maybe he does, but I am not so sure I do, not anymore. He isn't considering how changeable we are, how a new environment, a new job, a new friend, a new hobby can alter us to the point where we are no longer the person you remember. Context matters. Circumstances can be definitive. I knew all along he'd let me go. I counted on it, and I knew he'd put on a brave face because he couldn't deal with a version of himself that would be jealous and make me miss out. He'd rather lose me. I always loved that about him, and once thought I was the same, but now I see it is foolishness. I'd never have let him go without me. Oh, I assured him it wouldn't change me, but I knew even then that I was probably lying—and once that door opens, it cannot be closed, and now I am here in northern California, the fog banks obscuring the road back to Chicago.

THE GREAT
GILGAMESH

22

"Divorce? Wait. When?" asks Em.

"We haven't told Lilly, yet"

"Oh, no."

"Pretending everything is normal is killing me."

"I'm so sorry."

"The only thing that is making it bearable is the fact that Lilly hasn't noticed, I don't think. That kid is so damned smart, I can't be sure." I swallow a sob. "I never thought Ian would actually do it."

"What happened?"

I explain to Em about the night I ambushed him, how he began to sleep in the guest room, how we ignored each other for weeks after. It was so easy. Our lives really were separate. He left us, just like that. I opened a door he thought was closed and then he realized it'd just be easier to walk through it. Our life meant that little to him. We played pretend for a while and then one day I simply said, "You need to move out." He paused as if he was going to say something and then nodded. Then, I'm not embarrassed to admit, I threw a half-full can of soda across the table at him. He calmly stood from his chair, blotted his shirt with a napkin and told me I should work out the details of the divorce. He said he didn't care and that he'd sign whatever papers and then left the room.

"That is horrible," says Em and hugs me while I cry quietly so Lilly doesn't hear, like I have been doing for weeks now. Crying in the bathroom. Crying by the side door and frightening the neighbor kids as they return home from sports or drama club or whatever it is they do. I've even started smoking again, which I haven't done since I was fourteen and was trying too hard to be cool.

"Is he moving out?"

"He said I could keep the house if I wanted it, not that I can afford it. There are so many things that need to be worked out. He hasn't found a new place yet. We still need to tell Lil, figure out the finances, redo wills. It's a huge mess."

We sit in silence because there isn't anything left to say. There is no solution, no way to speed up time, no way to get beyond the demands of the moment. The present is consuming all that was once wonderful about Ian and me, and there isn't a thing I can do about it. The present is a shark's mouth eating the future and the past as well, swallowing some memories whole, nibbling at the corners of others and making them sag, slobbering all over some and leaving them warped and gummy. I wake every morning and see only the patches of land between slaughters. Things happen to me, outside prediction, beyond reach, bloated like the roots of trees we loved as children. Nothing I love grows with the strength of weeds. Only weeds can grow among weeds.

I remember we had a garden our first summer. It may have been our first "first." Ian was not my first anything: not my first kiss, my first love, my first time—all those rungs had been climbed long before he came into my life. He liked to ask me about my former girlfriends. I thought, at first, he was being a dude—being all worried that since I also liked girls that I was secretly gay and he was some kind of beard—but he wasn't that way at all. Like many, he could understand someone being into the same sex. That made sense to him even if it wasn't his cup of tea, but someone who was into anyone regardless of gender identification seemed to baffle him. He couldn't understand why I still called myself bi when I was in a pretty typical heterosexual relationship. I told him I was bi no matter who I was dating. I was bi even if I wasn't dating anyone. I don't need to cuff my jeans and throw up finger guns every ten seconds to prove my queerness. I'm bi and that is the beginning and the end of the story.

My freshman year in college, I met my first real girlfriend, a woman everyone called Carnage—no relation to the *Spiderman* villain. She was supposed to be this wild thing; that was her schtick, anyway. I mean, the theater department was a pretty weird place to begin with, subject to the ever-changing whims of the theater professors whose students followed their decrees like holy writ in their desperate search for the source of true art, so to be considered "wild" by these people had to count for something. I was in the music department studying sound engineering, but since we shared a building with the fine artists and the theater people, there was always some form of tomfoolery going on: half-naked models wandering about the upper floors, puppet shows in dark out-of-the-way corners, dance numbers in hallways. Flannel-clad guitarists played mopey songs in stairwells and clowns practiced their juggling routines in the bathroom mirrors. One semester a theater professor became obsessed with performance art and so caused a rash of happenings and flash mobs to occur at odd times during the day and night. One day I entered the Fine Arts building to find a friend tied to a chair and bound and gagged with electrical tape while a woman in sort-of bondage gear hacked away at his hair with a pair of what appeared to be very dull scissors. Most people walked by as if nothing very interesting was happening, waiting dully for classes to start. It's amazing what one can get used to. Or there was the time a theater student got shut down by campus security because he was attempting to recreate Chris Burden's "Shoot" but with a crossbow instead of a rifle. He called it "Bolt." "He was only going to graze my arm," the shirtless student pled as they confiscated the crossbow, security shaking their heads in consternation at the constant foolishness of undergraduates. The fact that no one got hurt or arrested was the real miracle of that year. There are some people the universe just protects. No matter what they get into, they always come out relatively unscathed. Their shells grow as extensions of their bodies with no effort or act of will. The shells are simply there when they need them. I, on the other hand, had to borrow shells and live in the constant fear of my meat growing beyond its bounds, knowing I'd eventually have to make another break for it, naked and revealed, for another borrowed shell—my one large asymmetrical claw useless against the fanged beaks circling above the tree line.

I met Carnage my freshman year; she was a junior. On the first day of lighting design class, which one of my professors suggested I take so I could make extra money doing lights for bands on the side, she entered the lighting studio wearing a sundress. It was the 90's and sundresses were totally in so long as you accessorized them with your favorite combat boots or cherry-red Docs. She walked in the door, saw me, and came right over and sat on my lap. She was not wearing any underwear. "And who might you be?" she asked half mockingly. I didn't know what to say, but I would come to find out that this was not uncommon behavior for her. I was saved by the professor walking in. When class started, Carnage went to her seat as if nothing much had happened. And to Carnage, nothing much had.

She had an apartment outside of town that was right on a little river where she'd throw parties. I think it was the Green River, like the band. Her claim to fame was that she owned a little boat—it fit maybe 5 or 6 people—which she'd use to cruise up and down the river. There were a few secluded spots we could go to drink a little, skinny dip, party. Normal stuff. One day, we were alone on the boat, laying in the shade of some trees, listening to The Sundays and smoking a joint when Carnage began kissing me. I would later learn that she often used The Sundays to seduce her lovers. It was her stock in trade. She started kissing me and I let her, not that I had a great deal of experience, but I was smart enough to play it cool. I had had flirtations in high school but nothing very serious. Even I wasn't daring enough to have a public relationship with a woman in high school. The 90's were not that cool. Carnage, for all her outward abandon, was actually quite tender and sweet. She wasn't a fool. She knew what she had on her hands, and she was delicate and kind and slow. There was something confident in her slowness. I liked that she was not in a rush. There are those who seem desperate to be done as if only the judgment of the performance mattered. There was something outside the moment and selfish about them. Of course, sometimes I liked too-eager too, when I could pretend all that eagerness was excitement rather than anxiety.

I had not thought of Carnage in years, but today I could use her reckless joy. Or maybe, I just want an available partner, or for sex to be as easy as it was when we were all much younger. Maybe I just wanted someone to want me again.

"Have you been going out on dates?"

"Actually, yes, a few." This seems to surprise Em, but she should know me better. As hard as this is, I am not going to sit here and wallow in it. If Ian is going to start a new life, then so am I. On weekend nights, I hand Lilly off to him and go out on boring dates with people I've met on OkCupid and Match.com. It is the most time he has ever spent one-on-one with our daughter, I am sorry to realize. I haven't made it past the coffee date with anyone—that's date number 1. "Does it get better? You have to tell me it does."

"It does not," says Em.

"I knew you were going to say that."

"I wish I could tell you something different, but it'd be a lie. Dating as an adult is ridiculous. You would think that spending the night would be the easiest thing in the world, right? Especially as an adult. I mean, it's not like being a teenager where you have to have sex in cars, or cemeteries, or worry every time you hear a sound that someone's parents are coming home early. But it's still an absolute nightmare."

"Were we ever teenagers?" I ask.

"We were never American enough to be teenagers, I don't think." I nod and Em says, "There are just so many things people in romantic comedies don't have to worry about."

"Like what?"

Here's something our companheira, Danielle Steel left out of her novels. When the sex is done and you're in someone else's bed, in someone else's place, with only one bathroom, which, for some reason, is always right next to the bedroom you are sleeping in, what do you do if you have to fart, or worse, to poop?"

"Oh my god," I say stumbling over a laugh. "I hadn't even thought of that."

"You have no idea how horrible it is to be wide awake while this strange person snores in your ear, your stomach roiling like a kettle, waiting for the moment they are all the way asleep so you can go let one rip in peace. But the second you move, they wake up because they think you might be making a break for it."

"You're killing me."

"Here's how you know your life sucks: when you find yourself at two in the morning, sitting in your freezing car, heat blasting, carpet-bomb farting and trying to come up with a plausible excuse for why you needed to go to your car in the middle of the night."

"Jesus," I say tears shooting out of my eyes.

"You have to take a hard look in the rearview when you find yourself in that place. Decisions were made. Bad ones."

"Oh, Em."

"I wish I was joking," she says and smiles.

"Can't we just get married?"

"I'm not the marrying kind, but I do love you."

"We could do two, simultaneous solo weddings."

"Not sure that would solve our problems. I wouldn't marry me."

"Anyone would marry you."

Ian and I had a garden our first summer. The next summer, only I had a garden. And then, there were no more gardens. I wanted to mourn losing him in the same way of devastation

I had loved him in during those long years, but this I wasn't sure I could do. I was happy to give when I loved him, but now I must take both our shares, all our shares, and save the devastation for myself. He cannot keep for himself what has always been mine to give or mine to keep, and if anyone is keeping the devastation for herself, it would have to be me.

EM DASH

23

CHICAGO 2017

"Please don't do this!"

"This has gotten way out of hand," says Pain Eyre crossly.

"This is the last one. I swear. Just one more, and I'm done."

"That's what I'm worried about, Em."

"I'm calling this off," says Silvia Wrath.

"No, they will be here any second. I can't back out now."

"This is dangerous."

"So is driving a car."

"Oh, please, don't give me that," Sylvia Wrath says, looking at me in the way a favorite but disappointed teacher looks at you when you try to con them. A knock at the door interrupts our discussion. I'm annoyed at Wrath and Pain but, in their defense, I didn't tell them in advance I had changed the rules, that I had decided to do this duel without any protective gear. I wasn't sure I'd be able to find anyone willing to duel under these conditions, but, once again, it wasn't that hard at all. After what happened the last time, I know this is the only way I can be satisfied, the only way any of this makes any sense or has any value. I admit I'm a little scared. It hadn't really occurred to me to be scared the last two times. Somewhere inside, I knew I wasn't going to die in those previous duels.

153

But this time, the possibility is as real as it is ever going to get, though dying is beside the point, I think. The point is for something to be exactly what it is and nothing more or less.

My opponent enters the room and we skip the pleasantries. We quickly agree on terms, ready ourselves and take our spots in the list. If I die here today, it will be worth it, I tell myself. Though I have no intention of being buried in a cemetery or having a funeral, I enjoy the thought of Gilga having to explain during my eulogy that I died during a sword duel. What would my stupid parents think? The thought makes me chuckle and earns me another glare from my seconds. But then I think about not being there to watch Lilly grow up, and my amusement turns to sadness—one deep enough it surprises me. Am I abandoning that little girl to a world that will not make easy room for her? Will she remember me? Am I any better than my parents? No, I can't think this way. She has her mother, a woman who will make sure Lilly grows strong and powerful. She will teach her that a ball and a chain are for drowning your foes, that a wedding ring is for sealing away evil spirits, that a lover must be sword and shield at the same time. She doesn't need me hanging around, poised and ready to run all the time. How many times have I made a run for it, made the act of leaving a definitive one? Too many times to count. And each time I managed to hurt only those who loved me most and not the ones who set me on the road in the first place. Lilly is not my blood but the thought that she will not remember me burns.

My opponent comes without seconds; she claims she doesn't have anyone she trusts enough to bring with her. She warns me that she has won a few tournaments. She doesn't want any misunderstandings. I appreciate her honesty, I tell her. If this were a tournament, I would not have much of a chance of beating her, but in a contest of attrition, where small injuries and other kinds of damage can make a big difference, I might have a chance, like when I was a kickboxer. In the gym, when faced with a superior opponent, my goal was to do as much damage as I could to their front leg, trying to equalize the gap in skill or size with raw toughness. In the movies, sword fights go on forever so long as the blades are clanging against one another but end rather quickly once steel hits flesh. In reality, an individual can take quite a bit of damage—even in critical areas—and continue to fight. I might be able to wear her down with my cardio alone. I had realized during sparring sessions that my extreme cardio background from derby and kickboxing gave me a huge advantage in longer, drawn-out matches or in contests at the end of the night when everyone else was tired. One very tall novice with a reputation for sparring too intensely found this out the hard way as I wore him down to the point where he stopped mid contest and said, "You are relentless," and then walked off the floor mixing deep respect with hilarious exasperation.

"*Salute,*" says Sylvia Wrath. We move into position. "*In guardia,*" and we both get into our stances. "*Pronti. A voi.*" We make a few passes with nothing much happening. Neither person wants to overextend and get caught with a counter. I can tell she is testing my distance and reaction time. She hasn't actually attacked, yet. My strategy is to lull her to sleep by doing everything in a predictable rhythm and then varying that rhythm at the right moment to catch her off guard. This is also a technique I learned from kickboxing. My coach explained it as a form of narrative, a way of telling your opponent a story. What he meant was that you could establish a certain set of expectations in terms of distance, timing, or rhythm and then break those expectations when it was most advantageous. However, I do not manage to fool her. Either she was waiting for it or I am so obvious in my approach that she reads my attack easily. She swats my rapier with her off hand and before I realize what is happening she hits me straight in the face with the hilt of her rapier and sends me crashing to the ground. Here's something I never dealt with in sparring. My seconds rush to me and my opponent backs off to her spot.

"Fuck, I told you. I told you. Are you ok?"

"I'm fine. I'm fine."

"Yeah, you look it."

"That's it. I'm calling this before it goes any further."

"No, you are not," I say. "This is not over."

"Look at your face," says Wrath.

"It's not a big deal. I've broken my nose before. I'll live."

"This is over. I'm your second, and I can call this off. Those are the rules."

"I said, no. Back off. I'm doing this." We stare at one another for a moment. Wrath is pissed and Pain looks like she is having a panic attack. She begins pacing frantically, taking deep breaths and doing something that looks a little like jazz hands in an effort not to lose control. I am sorry to worry my friends. They are derby girls. They have seen blood and broken bones. They know what is a serious injury and what isn't, but I know how this must look to them. But I have to finish this or I'll never be free of it. To be always under the sway of wonder is like having an itch that cannot be scratched, a question that begs to be answered but remains blinking like a cursor at the end of a line.

I get back up and wipe my nose on my sleeve. Blood. No big deal. A broken nose is nothing. I've broken my nose three times in my life. This just makes four. "Let's go again," I say, and spit blood onto the concrete floor. I know not to blow my nose so my face doesn't swell and block my vision. My opponent nods calmly and gets into her stance. For the next few passes, I manage to hold my own, even pulling off a pretty stylish left-foot *girata*, which looks like a bullfighter's move, to void a very quick thrust to the heart. She's not messing around now. With my defense holding, I try to make her move as much as possible, feinting over and over to make her lunge, seeing how long I can keep her holding that sword point out. These swords get heavy quickly. But I can't find any openings. Her movements are swift and efficient and she closes off the line of attack the moment I switch from inside to outside or vice versa, and now she is ready for any off-tempo attacks. I gave it away too soon. That could be a costly mistake. She is not tiring as I had hoped either. My only chance is a counter, but she is not someone to attack recklessly. It is a game of patience now. The person who loses their focus first is going to eat some steel. She finally commits to an attack; I see it coming so I close the line, but in my eagerness to parry, I get into a false time (leading with my foot instead of my sword point) and she sticks me right in the bicep before my sword is in the correct place. My arm seizes and searing pain shoots up to my shoulder, like grabbing a burning pan. I stifle a yell and grasp at the wound. At the edge of my consciousness, I hear a door scraping open against the concrete floor and look up just in time to see two police officers enter the room.

THE GREAT GILGAMESH

24

He may not pretend to find enlightenment or solace where there is none. He may not claim my body or my bones when I die like he always told me he would; he may sunder no part of me, stall no moment in the verb tense we once shared. Did he know the little African clawed frog could sing, the one we bought for Lilly's fourth birthday? It never made a sound before the day he abandoned us. It must not have started composing its evening song until he was gone. Obviously, it knew something I did not. How long did it linger beneath the water holding back the effort of its great breath, which is river and lake, which is ocean and salt nagging in from the east covering impossible distances to remind me I am not yet come home? In this house are sown the seed roots of my past, but it refuses me a place to bog my body in, not a tombstone but an eyepiece, a hag stone with a view of his back as he walks away over and over again like a creature of terrible sleep. I could sleep here—a crocodile at water's edge, its eye lazily scanning the watering hole, or a hippo whose titanic mass belies how quickly it can move in the river water.

I think of Manny in California. I think of Em and her grand disappearing act when we were children, of all our failed disappearing acts. I think of Ash who did not find what anger drew him towards in the west—only the disappointment and failure in the songs of his favorite loser heroes. I think of how he returned years later to Somerset bone tired and on his way to ruin, real ruin, not the teen kind. It was not the kind he knew before he left, where ruin meant fists and petty theft and breaking curfew.

Ash is in prison now, says his mother to mine, for impersonating a police officer and sexually assaulting a girl. How did my mother hold her face? Was it, like this? Like a lie? Or was it, like this? Like a shark's permanent smile? He was always an asshole, but was his heart always a predator or did he coax it out from its cave with impotence and listlessness? His mother said he'd started doing drugs—the oldest excuse in existence, maybe. What breaks inside a person that makes them want to hurt someone in such a way? It makes me fear that which wants to destroy what it cannot possess, what it cannot contain or drown.

Oh, my Tori, get me through this. Show me your "hiding place when spring marches in." The woman I am meeting is already ten minutes late. This is our second date and she's been late both times. She was an hour late for our first date. An hour! A lifetime. An extinction event. I have been sitting here like a moron drinking whiskey and getting angrier and angrier while the poor bartender tries his hardest to make me feel less foolish and alone by talking music with me. I don't even know how we got on the topic. He is young, too young. To him, the bands I like are lame, stuff his parents listen to. For me, the 1990's seem like only a few years ago. If I had any self-respect, I would leave right now. If only magic, if only goodness, if only the things we say, if only the promises we make, if only the things we do, if only they mattered. These are going to be hard lessons to learn.

I was seconds from bailing on our first date when she finally arrived. I was so angry I told myself I was only hanging around to tell her off, but then, she sat down, dressed in a little black dress and an elegant red shawl that made her look like Amalia Rodrigues and gave me this crooked smile full of winter that froze my anger. She apologized profusely, came up with what sounded like a plausible excuse about her daughter hiding a boy in the attic, and I forgave her instantly. It sounded like her teen daughter was a handful. If there was one thing I understood, it was how kids can warp space and time. Tori save me from Lilly's teen years. I did a sign of the cross just in case there was still any power in that gesture. But, here she was, late again. Fool me once …

In my youth, I would not have put up with this. As a young woman, I could sit in a corner of the room, ignore everyone looking my way, and they'd come find me. Unless Em was with me, then I might as well have been invisible, not that I minded—most times. The less effort I put in, the more they wanted me. It was that simple. And look at me now. Here I am, waiting again because she has the face of the women of my mother's village, though she is not one of our own. It is a face that knows how to look at the sea and wait, a face always in preparation for drowning and loss, a face for sailors and fishermen and songs so sad you cannot bear to look or turn away. Her crooked smile bending only just—a hint of brine and caldeira in it. It's too bad her best self is a swarm of bees, an apiary that acknowledges only its own sense of order. What absurdities would she invent for me this time? I do like stories, especially those with the flavor of truth. What if she gives me that sidereal smile again? Will I lose my strength and bend my will to hers? Is this what life is now? All compromise, which is another word for defeat. And for what, some awkward sex and me stealing away to sit in my car at 2 AM to listen to Mazzy Star and cry? Maybe after 40 all that is left is something that longs and longs.

GOMEZ ADDAMS

25

Manny is gone. I have to accept this fact. I can still remember how he looked the first time in his dorm room, the long slim lines of his body and his penis in my mouth—my first but I hoped not my last—the Cock of Barcelos, I thought at the time and nearly started laughing. And Manny's languorous movements as if he were without care or rush, as if he were some underwater plant that had never known the rhythms of dry land. I have loved so few people in my life: Manny, my grandmother. Not sure if that is sad or admirable. My grandmother—the woman who raised me until I was six—believed I could see like she could. My grandmother's power was well known in the little fishing village my family came from, but it seems her magic, as magic is wont to do, skipped a generation—missing two daughters and two sons—and landed on me. I often wonder in moments when superstition rises up in my heart, if her great power came at the cost of those two sons and a husband. She outlived them all by a large margin. The men in my family die young, age prematurely all at once and turn to wood for making boats to ply the dark Atlantic or for making fire on clear nights. But the women live deep into their 90s. She lost one son in a freak school yard accident and another in middle age due to heart disease. The men she loved most were long gone. The husband who chopped wood for the wood stove, the son who never became a man, the older son who opened a convenient store and then two more and was a great success—they were gone, but there was me.

My parents were young when I was born, had to work too many hours, and lived in a tiny third-story tenement in the city of immigrants, Fall River, so my grandmother offered to take care of me until they could get on their feet. And in so doing, she gained a third son—a child who from the start seemed like one of the creatures lurking in the Atlantic surf—a son my mother would never be able to reclaim for herself. This has always been the way of changelings and is the story my grandmother chose to tell about me. Some get to tell their own stories; others have stories thrust upon them. She filled my head with spirits, curses, mists—maybe to make up for how little we had. Who needed a new bike when you could command waves and wind? Who needed a Disney vacation when I could raise mists to protect the family from those who would harm us, like the neighbor boy I ripped off his bike and smashed to the street for throwing rocks at my sweet grandmother. Magic, as everyone knows, comes with a price and it seems it is either soaked in blood or drenched in irony—or both. I do not know if my grandmother's long life is the result of her own great power or of a spell I cast as a child—a bargain I made with whomever was listening. I did not want to exist in a world without her, so I offered up the second half of my life so that she would never leave me. My spell had been cast and it bound me to my grandmother forever and locked her to the land while I still walked it. It was a piece of dangerous witchery.

But anyone who works magic knows to fear the multiplied backlash; you must anticipate everything your will can bring forth or you will find yourself at its mercy. You will find yourself at its mercy in any case. I, being a child, did not anticipate well, did not know that Faustian deals are always tricks, or maybe I did and just didn't care, which is often how these things really go no matter what people say afterward. I asked only for her long life and that I got; she is 94. My grandmother's great power could not protect her from Alzheimer's, however, and I have been forced to watch her great light slowly dim for almost two decades. I should have made conditions, written in some fine print. She does not know me anymore, which is a savage piece of cruelty. And that isn't even the worst part. The worst part was how easy it was for me to walk into my adult life, how easy it was for me to move on and move away from the woman who loved me above all things. I do not know whose magic binds her to this world—mine or her own—but I hope the spell breaks soon, though her death fills me with a dread and a sorrow no less harrowing than the one I felt as a child. There is no person who anchors me to the past so much as she does and her loss will take something from me, but I give it freely. Take it! Only go and find where your spirit has gone to wait our coming. I cannot keep you bound here, locked in a mind that does not know itself, locked in a body that no longer answers to a will once so strong it held the entire clan of my family iron bound.

The story my family tells about me is one marked with the uncanny. Everyone said I knew things a young child couldn't or shouldn't know, which isn't the same thing. They said I was a little old man, born ancient and tethered to the deep. I like the story, but I think it was probably the result of growing up at the end of the Cold War and knowing the world could end at any second, that adults could destroy everything before you had a chance to actually live in it and not care one jot. It might not have been magic. It sounded more like the cold, hard whetstone of reason to me, but being thought a change-ling has its advantages.

When I was a child, I admit, however, to hearing whispers which seemed to warn me of danger or give me hints of the future, especially during storms. They weren't words in any real sense, though. It was a kind of background murmuring that would get louder or softer depending on the situation—mur-murs not of waves as much as the touch of a hand slipping in and out of reach. I chased the whispering, hoping to grab the future on its way by. I searched in the cacophony for the voice of my grandfather who died when I was 9, forever bookmarking 1986 in my heart. If anyone would know, it would be him, but I never did hear it. I wanted to stand in the presence of god, know the word that was action, though I never really believed such a creature existed. He was too convenient, and my small experience told me that is not how the universe really worked.

Then in college I began to hear my name called out in earnest. It's the only word I ever heard cut clearly through the mumbling: my name. How dull. How disappointing. This one thing I already knew, better than anyone else, my name. Even-tually, a doctor would give me pills to turn the noise down real low, though never turning it off altogether. As a child, I was very volatile. My family made excuses. Being tethered to the before is not without consequences, they reasoned. There were times when I was utterly beset by paranoia, feeling like everyone, especially my closest friends, were out to get me, but the meds eventually put a stop to most of that too. The best part, by far, was that I could sleep for the first time in my life. How terrible to be without sleep, how it tantalizes with promises of rest, with a break from being oneself. Before medication, I would lay there night after night, sleeping only when my body could no longer fight itself off, and it never felt like sleep at all. I'd toss and turn for hours as my brain spun its wheel without promise of gold, like Rumpelstiltskin's madness for a child he could not have. Nothing worked. Nothing helped. As a teenager, I took to stealing Valium from the medicine cabinets of my friends' mothers, just a few here and there so they'd never notice. Taking Prince Valium to bed helped me relax, but he did not help me sleep much.

One night, when I was home for break my sophomore year in college, my parents found me naked at 3 AM, all my furniture in a giant pile in the center of the room like I was building a funeral pyre, the walls covered in butcher paper and written within an inch of their lives in various colored markers. I hadn't built the spider's web of red yarn pinned into baroque designs that so often accompanies popular dramatizations of madness in the movies, but the effect was similar. I hadn't slept in a month. When they gently asked what I was doing, I told them I was writing a play—a play about the history of the world. They told me later—because the next day I could not remember much of what I'd said—that I had planned it to be a giant cycle that would take 72 hours of straight, nonstop performance to complete, that no one had ever done something so vast and it was going to make me the most important playwright since Shakespeare. It didn't matter that I had never written a play before. I would overcome all of that through sheer determination and desire. They said I was talking so fast I was slurring my words. I jumped from topic to topic, from idea to idea as if plugged directly into the matrix of the universe itself. And then two days later, I crashed. I had just had my first manic episode—a minor one—and now it was time for the depression. My parents called it "nerves" and blamed it on too much reading. Maybe they were right.

But as long as I took my meds and didn't push myself beyond certain limits (because I could), I was pretty stable and I quickly realized that stability, though not particularly sexy, was powerful. Contrary to the notion that an artist must suffer to create his best work, I found I did far better work when I didn't waste so much time and energy being anxious or paranoid or unable to get off my couch. My school work blossomed. The only problem is that I, like so many bipolar people, like the mania. It is thoroughly good. For a short time before the crash comes, before your thinking gets muddled and you stop making sense, before you destroy everything around you, you are in fact smarter than your smartest self, braver than your bravest self, and have the kind of energy that would tire out a six-year-old. It doesn't last long but during that short time it feels like the universe is a good place, a place infinite and yet possible, and that you are someone capable and daring enough to embrace those possibilities. But the price is too high to pay: weeks, sometimes months, sometimes more, unable to function, of hearing nothing but the hole at the center of all things yowling.

Since Manny's departure for California, I've been thinking about those whispers again, and my desire is growing for those spirits' partial voices making certainty where only uncertainty is now. It has been a long time. I need to know what awaits me. I need someone to call my name. Will the desert sands take the man I love? For the first time in my life, I have stopped taking my pills. Those of us with bipolar are notorious for thinking we are better and going off our meds, only to find too late we are not. And sometimes in those moments, marriages end, jobs come crashing down, bank accounts go empty, and friends disappear. I know my medications have saved my life, but that only matters when you have a life worth saving. You don't need magic when things are going your way. But now things are dire. For a week, nothing: no whispers, no signs, no portents. Dread grows in me. Two weeks, nothing. Maybe I am too far from the source. Maybe my powers grow weaker the farther I get from the Atlantic's dark bosom. Maybe I have frittered them away because I feared them and now they will not come in my time of need. If you turn away from your visions often enough, they stop coming.

The silence is a darkness without shape or limit. It is almost beyond endurance. Day after day like a weed without a challenge, with too much open space and light and water. And then, just as I am about to give in to despair, I hear it, suddenly, nothing but a wisp, but it is my name—not the name people know me by but my real name, the name I inherited—a rooster crow at the wrong time of day. And it cocks its head ever-so-slightly and says, *Don't let the silence fool you. It is not your hand that drums.*

THE GREAT GILGAMESH

26

I ate glass last night. My jaw's unhinged now and not in a good way. I know my dentist is going to push for braces big time. Every single time I go, she suggests I consider Invisalign. My teeth may not be America straight—our parents couldn't afford fancy orthodontics—but I'm not going to be one of those adults. I just can't pull it off. Some adults can be adorable in that way of innocence, but not most of us. All future partners will have to accept me snaggle-toothed or not at all—like Jewel. My daily Match.com routine is failing miserably to distract me. These profiles reveal nothing. Everyone says the exact same thing and it's so easy to see the lies. All the men my age want younger women. The young ones do too except for those who want a mommy, but I'm nobody's incest fantasy. Most of the people here are straight. I have to go to HER to find women to date, but no matter how many times I say I want to take things really slow, I keep getting booty calls. Why are all of these people in such a rush? I have not had sex with anyone but Ian for years, and with no one at all in the last six. I wouldn't even know where to begin. These are people who seem very comfortable with sleeping with strangers. What if they smell weird?

I've been listening to Hole at full blast all morning, stomping around my house looking for something to trample on like Liv Tyler stealing beauty in the Italian countryside. This is going to be a very bad day. If there was some way I could avoid doing what needs to be done, I would. I keep hoping the dormant super-volcano under Yellowstone will blow so I do not have to live beyond the next few moments. I could watch calmly as ash descends, its mothering arms enfolding the sun. I'd be sad not to see Lilly grow up, but, at least, she'd never have to know the truth of this day, which will be seared in her mind forever. I need Courtney Love's anger to cloak me. I've been staring at that pic of me crowd surfing at our last high school gig way back in 1995 for days now. Courtney Love did an interview after Kurt committed suicide where she described jumping into the audience to crowd surf at a gig and these fucking bastards start literally ripping off her clothes and basically sexually assaulting her right out in the open. All these angry little turds blaming Courtney for Cobain's death; all these little turds trying to claim Kurt wrote the songs on *Live Through This* because they were "too good." All these fragile little wretches who don't like it when the story doesn't fit their vision of the world. There is always someone who thinks they can take things from you. It didn't slow Courtney down a jot, her leg hitched up on her monitor like she was ready to kick your teeth in, by turns sweet and vicious, pretty and dangerous. Courtney is a knife ready to be wielded, and I need to be that girl now more than ever, the one who can still throw herself into a crowd.

Ian should have been home half an hour ago. He was supposed to meet me here at 5 PM so we could tell Lilly about the divorce together. I already puked once today and I feel like it might happen again. I can't remember the last time I threw up. I mean, I got nasty food poisoning last year and didn't puke a drop. It came out in droves, don't get me wrong, but only one way. On this of all days, Ian is going to arrive late, or maybe not at all. He'll say it was work; he'll say he couldn't help it. One more time, one last time, and I am free of him forever, though free is not the word I would use for how I am feeling at this moment. It is more like being bound to an absence, being bound to the idea of a person who no longer exists and who makes you question if he ever existed in the way you thought. Ian is around my neck; Ian is an albatross. I am Tori's Flying Dutchman: "Take a trip on a rocket ship baby where the sea is the sky."

It is 6:30 and still no Ian. I text. I call. I email. Nothing. I DM. I should have known. He will not come. That is how little we mean to him. He's leaving me, as always, to do the hard work myself. Lilly is finishing her bath and getting ready for her night-time routine of watching TV on the couch with me.

"Lilly, put on your PJs, ok?"

I hear her running to her room, most likely leaving a swath of soaked footprints from the bathroom. This child cannot seem to understand the function of a towel. And for some reason, Lilly can't just take out one pair of pajamas. When I come upstairs, it's like her dresser has erupted, like the PJs could no longer contain themselves and were just waiting for her to return to have a wild rumpus in her room—and maybe they were. My stomach flips again. I rush to the toilet but nothing comes out, just a silent grimace without release. All of my muscles are stretched to their limits.

"Lilly, honey," I manage to say, "come downstairs, please."

"Can we watch *iCarly*?"

"Sure, but first I'd like to talk to you." Lilly doesn't like the tone. She looks at me like she's in trouble, but she's smart enough not to give anything away, just in case. "Sit next to Mommy," I say patting the couch and she does, eyes wide and feet poised ready to flee, her hair wet and matted to her head and neck. "You're not in trouble, but there is something I need to discuss with you." I have to pause and take a sip of water. My throat will not clear and my hands are shaking so hard I'm afraid to drop the glass, but I cannot live one more day like this, and Ian will not come. He will not come to save me and make this day not happen. Like all the women in my family, I am left to do the dirty work. Everyone else just does what concerns them, but I am responsible for the whole show. And I thought I was escaping the sad fate of all those Portuguese girls from back home, married to the son of some family friend who you thought was your uncle or your cousin all your life, having cookouts in the backyard and being harassed to an early grave by a mother-in-law who thinks your house is never clean enough no matter how much you clean it, and a mother who comes over to do laundry and wash dishes like you are still in high school. Actually, that doesn't sound too bad to me right now. I'd love for someone to come over and wash my dishes and do my laundry, so I can find my feet on the ground again. My parents aren't far, but if I open that door, they will never let me be again. I can't open another door to let the monster in.

"Do you know what divorce is?" I say softly in an unbearably rehearsed manner because I've been practicing this speech in my head for weeks so I don't start crying. I must not cry. I need to show Lilly we'll be ok. Her eyes grow wider, if that's possible, and she nods once very slowly, grimly. "Look sweetie, Mommy and Daddy have decided it would be better if we didn't live together anymore …" but before I can get any further, Lilly starts crying and repeats the word, "no" over and over as if there is a certain number of repetitions that will make it so, that will take back what has just been said. I can't blame her. I have been doing the same thing in my mind since the separation. It hasn't worked any better for me.

"When are you going to get back together?" she manages to ask between no's.

"We're not, baby. That's not how it works."

She begins repeating the word again, fingers in her ears now and eyes closed against an implacable certainty, spinning like she always does when her feelings get too big.

"I'm sorry, Love. I wish it wasn't true."

"Why? Why? I don't want to be divorced."

"You aren't divorced, honey. Mommy and Daddy are. We're still your parents. We'll always be your parents. We'll always love you."

"Will we still be a family?"

I admit I wasn't prepared for this one and I don't want to promise her things that won't happen. "No, honey. We will always be your parents, but we aren't a family anymore." And this starts another round of "no's" and I want so much to just cry and cry and never stop. But I must help Lilly. She is all that matters.

"Why are you doing this?"

"I'm not doing this, Sweetie. It isn't what I want, but sometimes Mommies and Daddies grow apart," I say, repeating the party line of every divorced parent ever. I am a cliché. Lilly cries some more and I can do nothing so I hold her. When Lilly finally calms down some, I explain to her how it will work, that she will have two houses now, two bedrooms, two Christmases and birthdays. Two families instead of one. In spite of herself, she likes the idea that she is actually getting more instead of less. My strong girl, who can find something to hold onto when I can't. Well, no, that's not quite true. I hold onto her. She is all that matters to me now. I wait for her to fall asleep in my arms and put her to bed. It is over for now, over except for the incontrovertible fact of living it.

Time passes without me noticing, my stomach so full of burrs and thistles I don't notice when I nod off. Then I hear the key turn in the door and jump back into wakefulness as if falling into it. I cannot believe Ian has the balls to show up now. This is my final sortie. I give no more ground. My back is to the sea and I must fight to the end and fight I will.

"I'm sorry. I couldn't get away any sooner," he says before I can say anything.

"I don't care."

"G., please. I did my best."

"You bailed on me again, like you always do. Your best isn't worth a damn." I pause and take a breath so he will hear me plainly. "You made me do it alone."

"I know. I was hoping you'd wait for me."

"No, you weren't. That's why you never responded to any of my messages. You were hoping I'd get tired of waiting and do it for you, which is exactly what happened. Well, you got your way, so now it is time for you to leave."

"I'm sorry. I'm sorry," he says again, smaller than I have ever seen him before. I decide right there that when I'm beyond this moment, I will remember him like this. This will be the last sweet thing I associate with his memory, but right now I am mad as hell.

"Give me your key," I demand and hold out my palm. Ian looks at me like he is going to resist but then unwinds the key from the ring and hands it to me. "You abandoned your daughter, tonight," I say, calmer than I've been all day. For the first time, he actually looks sad but that starts to make me angry again. And yet, some deep, deep part of me wants to reach out to him, wants to hold him like only I can and admit how hard it has been and how unfair it all is, but I can't. I want to say I will never forget what we were, but I don't. I will make myself forget. It is my one play. He didn't pick us. I asked him to pick me and he didn't. He didn't pick Lilly.

"Can I just kiss Lilly goodnight?"

For a second, I thought he was going to ask to kiss me, and my heart shatters to even smaller pieces. Every part of me wants to say no. I crave ruthlessness, but I know it is futile. He only feels guilty in the moment. The second he is out that door, he will start to feel better like Neo eating the chocolate chip cookie in *The Matrix*. Some part of me is relieved he wants to see Lilly, another wants him gone now.

"Don't wake her up. And then, please, just go."

GOMEZ ADDAMS

27

Can't leave the couch. It's too much effort to move to the bed. Can't sleep, anyway, so it doesn't make much difference. A whisper whips by my face almost touching my lips, just my name again. Always the same thing. Who's calling? Not Manny. He cannot hear me. He's in California with the monstrous February roses blazing deep in the Tule fog, being carried away on the crisp yellow wings of a swarm of Alfalfa butterflies. My attempt to bring back our correspondence from our school days failed. I guess things like this don't matter now that he has the job he always wanted. He's not entertained anymore by silly emails about movies and TV shows, does not see the love letter hidden in my musings on Val Kilmer and pop culture. There was a time when he would have recognized a love letter when he read it, one hammered on an anvil, then sharpened and etched in acid. The more layers of steel and iron, the prettier the Damascus, the better the proof. Anyone can say, "I love you." Anyone can buy a sentiment off the rack, but it won't ever fit right. It'll always be a suit that sags and bags in the wrong places. They are good enough but never good. For our wedding vows, I chose a poem about a divorce. Everyone thought I was nuts (everyone except Manny), but in that poem was all the grit and dirt and damage necessary to make a marriage, a true marriage. I would choose the love of dirty sinks and boredom and failure over the love of car radio songs any day. But if my marriage fails, everyone will say I had it coming. Like in *The Crow* when the main characters are killed and a cop asks, "Who gets married on Halloween?" and kindly Officer Albrecht responds, "Nobody." Brandon Lee was one of ours, I hear Manny say, but it isn't true. Brandon Lee isn't Portuguese, or maybe he is.

Manny sends short emails promising to write back but never does. My name bounces off a wall and ricochets around the living room. It's pointless trying to triangulate its origin. It's not coming from where I want it to, nor is it going anywhere beyond the walls of this room. Nor am I. I tried going to work, but I'm staying home more than I'm going in. Not sure how many sick days I have left. Like most Americans, I almost never take sick days, even when I'm sick—maybe especially when I'm sick—which from this spot on my couch seems morally wrong. The television rattles off some Netflix show of the moment I can barely pay attention to. The words don't seem to stick. I can hear them but they're gone a split second later. Fast cuts make my eyes hurt. The apartment is a total mess. If Manny walked in the door right now, he'd be horrified because I'm supposed to be the neat one, but he won't, so who cares? I can see the top of a tree in the window. There's no wind. Nothing moves, like the world has decided to lay beside me on the couch like a corpse at a wake when we could still lay the dead in our homes, before they professionalized death and ruined it.

No word from Manny in weeks. He's been gone almost four months, off galivanting with his new friends. I'm just a reminder of snow and cold and ice. He's better off without me. We brought each other nothing but failure, anyway. When we were in school, everything seemed to be going according to plan. We had been careful to map out every move, make sure we didn't miss any steps. Most people seem to go about their days randomly. Even if they know where they want to go, they don't seem to have any clue how to get there, but not us. We had it all figured out. All we had to do was hang in there when things got tough and we'd win in the end. The long con, we called it. But that is not how it went. Or was it? Manny found the path, against all the odds (the odds he calculated and re-calculated obsessively for years), but, somehow, I got left out of the equation; somehow, I became the loser in the loser matrix.

Maybe I have always been the loser, living dangerously on borrowed time since the very beginning. I was born two months premature, which in the 70s was a death sentence. They told my parents to prepare. I was so small my father said he could hold me in the palm of his hand. They said I'd die, so my parents did not give me a name, but I didn't die. Then the doctors said I'd be small and sickly and likely not last too long, and my parents found a name in their hearts but did not speak it. And I lived. My first experiences of life were in death's great black palm. I had chances, had every excuse, but my little weed's strength was stronger than death's subtle whispers in my ear. He cooed to me, enclosed me in the folds of his ancient and familiar cloak, which was soft and not tattered and rough as it appears in the movies, but I would not tell him my name and so his power could not reach me. But he has held my other hand all my life, sweetly and patiently. I do not now nor have I ever feared him for the look on his bone-aged face has always been one of concern and love. Death plays no tricks. He has no need of them for we shall all come unto him in our true time.

The tree outside does not move: nothing on its dead branches, no leaves to flutter, no tough winter birds shrugged against cold. Another whisper. My name. Who is calling? It's not my grandmother. She is lost, trapped between worlds. It's not Manny. This is my life now. I am so tired of it all, so bored with myself. Why should I have to do this anymore if I don't want to? No one is here to stop me. No more desire for things I can't have. No more three-hour car rides. No more stupid job, no more stupid meetings. Finally, the peace and quiet that is without yearning, the dark that does not long for a single other thing. I've had a bottle of pills next to me for a few days now. I know why they are there. I know what they are for. I put them there, after all, though I admit I don't know exactly what they will do to me, but if one makes me sleep through the night, maybe an entire bottle's worth will make me sleep until the world finally comes to its proper end, the long hard hug at the end of night, the embrace that never lets go.

EM DASH

28

I look over in time to see two very annoyed police officers enter the room. You know you live in Chicago when cops enter a basement to find people dueling with swords and their response isn't surprise or anger but annoyance. After I got smashed in the face with my opponent's guard, Pain Eyre called the police. I don't blame her. She thought she was doing the right thing, but the truth is we might all be going to jail tonight. Though spending a night in a cell would make this a truly kickass story, I don't relish the idea of having to do it. I imagine my answer to the question, "What are you in for?" will probably beat all comers. Isn't that what always happens on TV? Some tough looking woman will ask the newbie what she is in for before taking her shoes or pushing her face in the toilet. The reality is likely a lot more boring, I hope, anyway. The cops look worn out, like new parents who find out only too late what it really means to be in way over their heads. They give us a thorough talking to and it seems to me they are either deliberately not saying what is going to happen to us or they aren't sure what to do. Apparently, there aren't any specific laws about fighting with swords, and since the only person hurt is me, they don't arrest us. Unless someone is willing to press charges, there isn't too much the cops will do, most of the time. He does confiscate our swords, however, which is a real bummer. My opponent's sword was a really nice one and though mine isn't anywhere near as expensive, I cannot afford a new one and the school swords are terrible. One cop does say, however, that if he ever catches us doing this again, he'll charge us with assault and battery, which is a felony. And then they leave, shaking their heads, maybe thinking the world is too stupid to deal with. I am not sure if it is relief I am feeling over not being arrested or disappointment. A little of both, I guess, but mostly relief.

Then my cell chimes. It is Gilga. She texts, "Call me immediately!" And my first thought is of Lilly.

"Gilga, are you ok? What's happened?"

"It's Gomez."

I am caught off guard because that is not what I was expecting her to say.

"Hello?" she says.

"Sorry, what? Manny's Gomez?"

"Yes, I just got a phone call from Rush Hospital," says Gilga.

"Why did they call you?"

"Don't know. Maybe he didn't want to worry Manny because he's in California."

"What happened?"

"I guess he gave them my number as emergency contact."

"That's really weird."

"Em, he's in the psych ward."

"He is? Wait, did he … ?"

"Don't know," she sighs. "They wouldn't tell me anything."

"Did you call Manny?"

"I did. He's jumping on a flight as we speak. He'll be here later tonight."

"Good," I say, relieved.

"Can you visit him and find out what's going on? I know it's a lot to ask."

"I will. I have to make a stop at the hospital, anyway."

"What?"

"Nothing. Nothing. I got this."

"Em, should I be worried?"

"No, it's all good."

"I'll let that go for now. Call me when you know something. Sorry to put this on you."

"Don't worry about it. It's not like you can fly in. I'll call you when I get some details. Is Lilly ok?"

"She's hanging in there."

"Did you tell her about the divorce?"

"I did. She cried. Kept asking when we were going to get back together. It was horrible. I haven't stopped crying for days. And, you know what? Ian didn't even show up."

"What the fuck! Are you serious?"

"Made me do it alone," says Gilga.

"God, I wish I could have been there."

"I know, me too. We'll talk more later. Go deal with Gomez."

"Ok, love you."

"Love you too."

Night descends, hiding the fissures in the ice, the crevices in the dirt, the cliff edges from the roadside—fissures whose bottom is frozen pond, crevices whose dirt is the desert at the depth of a sword wound, cliff edges that fall away from the ones we love most, lit only by the lightning flashes of emergency lights.

GOMEZ ADDAMS

29

CHICAGO 2017

Somehow, I always knew I'd end up here. Manny won't have to work too hard to rationalize leaving me, and that's ok. I don't want to drop this crap on him when things are finally going his way. The grogginess hasn't totally left me, though the memories of having my stomach pumped are very, very sharp and in focus, as is the pain in my right eye. With my good eye, I see a woman at the foot of my bed. Her nose looks smashed and her face is bruised and puffy, and she has an arm in a sling, blood staining the sleeve of her shirt. If this was a competition, she'd likely win. Even here, I am bested.

"So, you're she," I say.

"Am I?"

"The girl of Manny's dreams."

"I thought you were the girl of Manny's dreams," says Em.

"If only."

"Nice eye patch."

"Nice sling."

"Thanks. Want to sign it?"

"Isn't that usually reserved for casts?" Em raises an eyebrow in response. "Manny would be really upset if he knew you were here," I say.

"He's on his way."

"Is he? He's leaving his Californian paradise for little ol' me?" I say doing my best Doc Holiday southern drawl, "I'm honored." Em looks confused. She doesn't seem to know what to make of my sudden fall into a bad southern accent (and why should she?), so she keeps staring at me. I remember a scene like this one from when my grandfather was dying, except I am not dying—not this time, anyway. "I'm surprised," I say trying to get back on track, my brain still a bit addled.

"Why would you say that?"

"I don't seem to be very high on his priority list these days. He barely writes me back, and when he does, it's boring lists of what he's been doing with his new friends." It is the kind of note you send your mother when you go away to college, I think, not for the first time. It is little better than a Christmas card featuring a family you could care less about in matching ugly sweaters. There is nothing of substance in his messages. They are an act of violence. "I don't know what's happening to him," I continue. "I mean, he's playing racquetball and going to wine tastings in Lodi, because 'Lodi is the new Napa.' He actually fucking said those words to me and not ironically. He told me he's thinking of going in on a plot in a vineyard so he can make his own wine. Who is this person?"

"Maynard from Tool has a vineyard and makes his own wine."

"That can't be true."

"It is. Saw a documentary."

"Oh, well, ok, I guess it's not so bad then. But did you know he's playing again? Can you believe that? Years and years, I beg him to play for me again and nothing—always an excuse— but then he moves to California and he and 'Jonathan,'" I say flinging up wild scare quotes like gang signs, "are playing coffee shops and writing songs like it's no big deal."

"He's playing again?"

It is the first thing to really break Em's measure. "See? When I bring it up, he blows me off, says it doesn't mean anything, but we all know it's not true." It all came out at once. I have been holding these feelings in for so long. I was too scared to say them out loud before but now that they've come out I realize I'm really angry.

"How are you?" Em asks after a pause.

I shrug and consider saying, "Better," but better than what? If you couldn't dispatch with pleasantries in the mental ward, where could you do it? "What happened to you?" I ask gesturing at her ruined face.

"Broken nose. You?"

"I seem to have come down with a major case of myopia."

She gives me the beginning of a smile, the barest transition into a smile, and then stops at the crack in her lip from whatever collided with her face. "I can see that, though probably better than you can."

"Ah, an eyeball joke. Very good," I say. "My mother always warned me that I wouldn't be happy until I poked my eye out."

"She did?"

"No, my mother would say, "Bem feito," meaning, that's what you get.

"That sounds about right," she says and gives a real laugh. "Were you trying to gain knowledge of the runes or something?"

"Why not? I had nothing better to do."

"You went full Odin. Respect."

"Thanks."

"Did it work?"

"Actually, it did—sort of."

Em had disappeared the summer Manny and I started dating. I never got a chance to get to know her too well. I missed most of the band thing. She clears her throat like she is trying to decide if she wants to say something: "I know what you're going through. I know that's lame to say, but I've been there."

"Where?"

"Here. I mean, not here, but I've done this before when I was a kid."

"Really? Manny never mentioned it."

"He doesn't know. I never told him."

"Why tell me?"

"Well, look around. I know that's harder for you now but you'll get used to it."

"Oh, that's strike two," I say meeting her laugh, which dies down quickly and leaves us in the midst of another silence that wants to end but is afraid of what might be said next. "What happened?" I ask.

"I pulled a Chris Cornell."

"A what?"

"Pretty noose is pretty pain," she sang. "And I don't like what you got me hanging from," she continues, finishing the line from Sound Garden's "Pretty Noose"—a song where Chris Cornell foreshadows his own death, though it wasn't the only song where he used gallows imagery.

"I'm sorry."

"It was a long time ago."

"How come you never told Manny? Wasn't he your best friend?" Em pretends not to hear what I am saying. No, that's not quite right. She isn't pretending not to hear, she is simply letting me know she's not going to answer. "He went to all your bouts, you know. Never missed one. I kept telling him to just talk to you, that it was creepy to be stalking your games, but he couldn't do it."

"I know."

"You know?"

"Not the whole time. I saw him once. I figured it probably wasn't the only time."

"No, it wasn't. Why didn't you say something to him?"

"Why did you let him go to California?"

"Let him? What was I supposed to do, forbid it?"

"No, but you just let him go. Didn't even put up a fight."

"How do you know?"

"Gilga told me."

"So, wait, you're talking to Gilga but not Manny? That's fair."

"I didn't say it was fair. It just kind of happened."

"Well, California just kind of happened too. You've been talking to Gilga and Manny's been talking to Gilga, and she didn't say anything to Manny?"

"I asked her not to."

"You guys need to work on your friendship skills. I thought you were all supposed to be so tight—As Malcriadas, right?" I said more vehemently than I had intended to.

"I guess I fucked it up."

We sit in the hospital smells and beeping machines in other rooms.

"I guess I fucked it up too. Should I have tried to stop him?"

"Of course not. You can't stop Manny if he's decided to do something."

"Exactly."

"But that doesn't mean you just let him go and pretend like it's all good."

"Not sure what I could have done. I'm not going to beg him to stay. Either it's me or it's not me."

"Then you're going to lose him."

"Don't say that," I say feeling more fear than I have in some time.

"Not sure why it has to be only those two options."

"Look, had it been me who landed the job, I'd want to go too. I might have stayed if he'd asked me, but I would never have forgiven him for making me miss out. Not on purpose, but I'd have resented him for sure. I could not do that to him. I could not have that on my conscience. Does that make sense?"

"It makes perfect sense, actually. I would have done the same thing. Please don't tell Manny what I told you, ok Odin?"

"That's strike three ... but I won't."

"Want anything? Coffee, snack?"

I shake my head no. Em nods, pats my leg awkwardly, and goes to sit in the chair in the corner behind the door.

"How did you get in here, by the way?"

"Said I was your girlfriend."

"They're going to be a little confused when my husband shows up."

"Times have changed."

"Not that much."

How did I get here? It had to be 1986. It is the year everything went wrong. I was nine years old and it was already decided, already over. 1986: Optimus Prime dies in the first fifteen minutes of *The Transformers: The Movie*; 1986: my grandfather dies; 1986: Chernobyl melts down; 1986: Space Shuttle *Challenger* explodes in the face of every fourth-grader in America. Did Christa McAuliffe, with her small smile and blonde perm, learn the truth of fire? Or, did she survive long enough to learn about gravity and its jealous desire to reclaim its wayward children? My hero dead; my grandfather—the man who worked his whole adult life in a mill until cancer took a great big bite of his leg—gone, and the promise of other worlds derailed—decisions were made.

I must have fallen asleep because when I open my eyes it is dark out. The room is shadows and white institutional paint, and the clock reads 6 PM. Em is still in the corner chair reading a book. For some reason this makes me happy. I never really knew Em. I had only started dating Manny when she vanished. It isn't until this moment that I realize how much of an influence she has had on my life, not that she ever intended it to. Manny just couldn't seem to let her go, and I never knew why. Gilga should have been the one most directly affected; Em ran out on her at the exact moment their band got signed to a label, Manny told me. Manny, on the other hand, didn't seem too disappointed when the band called it quits. I was there. He had already moved on to what would become our life by then. And yet, he couldn't seem to let Em go, stalking her online for years before finding the derby team. There was something unfinished about that story. I wasn't sure if Manny knew what it was, or if Em was simply the name he gave to his unhappiness. Em's shade could embody all his dissatisfaction with his job, with me, with the universe. Em is someone to chase after because she dashes from place to place before you can find her borders. Em has always been the destination Manny could never reach. Em spares him the normal small-ness of arriving.

"Look at you. What did you do?" Manny rushes into the room, right past Em, who is partly-hidden behind the door. "You stupid idiot."

"I'm ok. I'm ok. Don't fuss."

"Your eye," he says reaching out to touch it but holding back at the last second.

"I'm fine."

"You're not fine. The nurse says you might never see out of that eye again. What happened?"

"What did they tell you?"

"Not much. Something about pills and then you blinded yourself?"

"I didn't blind myself. I took a bottle of Seroquel. I'm not even sure if you can OD on that stuff. I just wanted to sleep."

"Forever, though, right?"

"Yes, that's true," I admit unabashedly, and Manny looks on the edge of panic. "Forever, but then I chickened-out and called 911."

"What did you do to your eye?"

"The meds made me feel like I was going to barf, so I ran to the bathroom, but you know Seroquel makes me woozy. I don't remember much, just losing my balance and going down for the count. Apparently, I nailed my orbital on the toilet bowl as I fell. Totally KO'd myself. I didn't even feel it. It's so stupid."

"Why didn't you tell me?"

"Tell you what?"

"That you needed help."

"I didn't need help. I needed answers."

"Same difference, idiot."

"Well, I never claimed otherwise. You don't love me now that I'm a cyclops?"

"Gomez, stop. It's not funny."

"It is now that you're here, *Cara Mia*."

He shakes his head in disbelief and then hangs his arms around my neck. His kiss on my cheek is the first warmth I've felt in weeks.

"So what now?" he says, nervously.

"They want me to stay here a few days for observation, make sure I'm taking my pills correctly, that kind of thing. I have to call my boss. Shit."

"Don't think about that right now."

"I love you."

"I love you too, you stupid pirate."

"Oh, a pirate joke. So lame."

"You do look rugged with an eye patch."

"I knew I would."

Manny is quiet for a while. He holds me, but I can feel his breaths are shallow. Whatever he is thinking isn't pleasant, but there is nothing I can say to help, nothing that won't be a big fat lie.

"Gomez," Manny says softly, "are you ok? I'm scared."

"Don't be scared."

"How can I not be?"

"I know. I know. But listen, I'm ok. Today, I don't want to die. That's the best I can do."

"Jeez, babe. How did we get here?"

"I don't know," I say since it is all I can think of. "I'm tired. Can we talk more about this later?"

"Only if you promise that we will talk about it."

"I promise," I say and nudge my head towards the chair. Manny follows my good eye.

"Oh my god. Em? Is that? Em? What are you doing here?"

FROST HEAVES
EMMANUEL

30

"What are you doing here?"

"Gilga called me," Em says, motioning for me to follow her into the hall.

"My god, what happened to your arm? Is that blood? What is happening around here? I leave for a few months and everything goes to crap."

"It's nothing. I'm fine."

"I'm hearing that a lot today. Somehow, I'm not super convinced. It's nice to see you," I say after a brief, weird pause. Em doesn't respond, gives me that quizzical look she had mastered in elementary school, one that said she wasn't going to finish your thought. It'd be adorable if it wasn't exasperating. I don't know how to proceed. I've been waiting for years for this opportunity, but in all that time I had never figured out what exactly I was going to say to her. Here she was, my Em at long last, and no thoughts would come to my rescue.

"How's California?" she asks.

"It's good. Real good."

"Congratulations on the job, by the way."

"Thank you. I didn't think it'd ever happen." The bloom is still bright, and the roses wilder than I want to admit. My heart is still back in the desert though my mind is trying its hardest to remain in the present with Gomez, with Em, who I had hunted for years only to find her when I no longer expected to find her.

"Good. That's good."

The conversation doesn't know how to turn over. There is too much to be said and it is clogging the works. I realize, not for the first time, that whatever went down between Em and I is still utterly obfuscated. Maybe it is just too late in the day for one of these happy reunion episodes. Too much life has passed. We might as well be speaking across dimensions. "Uh, look, you can go if you want to. I've got this now. Thanks for looking after Gomez for me. If you want to, maybe we can get together another time, have coffee or something."

"Yeah, sure. Give me a call sometime. Gilga has my info," she says in that way we both know means we never will. If I let her go now, I'll never see her again. I'll never get to ask her why she left me, if it was something I did. "Em?" She pauses as if she is thinking of making a break for it, but then decides if this is going to happen it needs to happen now, and once and for all. "Did I do something? Way back when we were still in high school?" Em thinks, not in the way that indicates she is trying to find the right words for inchoate thoughts but in the way that measures whether it's worth saying words long rehearsed and prepared for.

"No, not really."

"You can tell me. I can take it."

"Everyone who says that, can't."

"So, I did do something. Just tell me then, and I won't bother you ever again. I promise. No more showing up at derby bouts."

"Manny, it wasn't just you. It was more complicated than that."

"Can you explain?"

"I'm not sure."

"Did I do something to make you quit the band?"

"No," says Em.

"Then why did you leave without a word?"

"It wasn't clear at the time. I didn't know it was our last goodbye. I just knew I needed to get away or everything would be decided for me before I had a chance."

"What does that mean?"

"Manny, you always told me what to think and how to feel. Even when I thought you were right, you forced me into things before I was ready."

"Like when? Give me an example."

"Like all the time. Remember in seventh grade when you convinced me there was no god?"

"Of course, but you admitted you had doubts already."

"Yes, I did, but you singlehandedly stole eternity from me before I was ready for it. I was 12, for fuck's sake. I would have come to it eventually, but you needed me to do it when you were ready, not when I was."

"But …"

"And you did this all the time."

"Like when?"

"How about telling me about sex when I was 6. Making me play Spin the Bottle in junior high so I could have my first kiss. Getting me drunk when I was 14 so we could see what it was like. All on your schedule. You never respected my boundaries. Calling my parents when I expressly said not to," she says after a brief pause to let me know that this was the greatest of the sins I had committed.

"You basically lived at my house, and we couldn't even meet your parents?"

"It's not the same. My parents are horrible."

"But you made that decision for us. We just had to believe you. How is that different?" I ask.

"I loved your parents, Manny. They were good to me. They were the ones I wanted more than anything."

"You never told me that."

"Your parents weren't perfect but they wanted you. If they did nothing else, they wanted you. Mine didn't want me, so they would not have given a crap about you and Gilga either. I didn't want you to see that."

"But what does this have to do with the band?"

"It's the same, Manny. Even the band was you. Gilga started the band, yes, but you were the one who made me join, who made me learn to play guitar so we could do it together. I loved being with you, but I didn't really want to be in the band."

"Why didn't you say anything?"

"Because there is no talking to you, sometimes. I'm sorry, but it is true. Do you know how much effort it would have taken for me to convince you you were wrong about something? So, yes, I took the coward's way out and just went with it most of the time. Do you know I hate Grunge?"

I admit that one stopped me dead in my tracks. It's like finding out you were adopted. "You don't like Grunge?"

"Not really. To be honest, I'm more of a Madonna, Cindy Lauper, Michael Jackson, Prince kind of girl. I love dance music. I love Paula Abdul, Bobby Brown. See?"

"Wow. I don't know what to say. Is that why you left the band?"

"No, my music tastes are beside the point. When we were offered the tour, I knew, somewhere deep inside that if I did it, my life would never change. I'd be doing what you wanted forever, or at least until you moved on to other things and left me holding the empty bag."

"I'm sorry."

"I'm not blaming you," says Em.

"God, I'm such a shit."

"No, you aren't. It wasn't just you, ok? It was all of you. You guys were exhausting. You have no idea how suffocating it is to be around people who always know what they want. It's what I loved about you, to be sure, but it was so hard to live up to—that iron sense of purpose. Even Ash knew what he wanted to be, and he's an idiot!"

"I see."

"Manny, do you remember what you said after you almost drowned? You said that the other children, the drowned ones, had a terrible desire to live, remember? That's what you said. They wanted to live! More than anything, to live."

"I've never felt anything like it. An awful desire."

"That's what it was like to love you all. You seemed so desperate to live and I could barely understand it. I still don't. And you wanted it for me almost as badly as you wanted it for yourselves. I tried my hardest to live up to it, but I never could. It was a lie, and that's why I left, at least I think so now. It was never this clear at the time."

A sadness stole in on me as I realized how little I actually knew about Em and not just because so many years had gone by. She has always been mostly mystery. It might be what drew us to her, but I never really stopped to consider what she was keeping from us and how lacking we were in curiosity. Beneath the ice, the others wanted to live. That was true. Above the ice, we wanted to live, more than anything. I wanted to live, so I assumed it was true for everyone I loved, not realizing that for some the ice is a warm soothing hand lulling you to sleep in the cracking silence at the ends of the earth. Like Em. Like Gomez? I felt I might fall over. If I were lucky, maybe I'd knock out my own eye and Gomez and I would have something new in common—a monocular world where only together would we be able to see clearly and in depth.

There seemed nothing more to say. It was finally here. The finished act—a tumble into the suicide seats. We hugged and even though I knew we'd likely never be friends again, it felt so good to be near her. She was right about us. I guess I always thought all those ambitions and plans were a good thing, that it was the only reason to be with us in the first place. I mean, what else did we have to offer? Nothing much. We were nothing, so we played that one song over and over again, hoping that in repeating it enough we could convince ourselves, and by extension the universe, of its inevitability. But in so doing, I pushed one of my best friends away from me forever and, worse, almost ruined her life with my selfish and tiny vision of what happiness is. And I wasn't done for the night. There was one more conversation that still needed to happen, one more consideration of happiness, one more probability to run—and it was in the next room pretending to be asleep, waiting for me to come back to him.

EM DASH

Epilogue

We salute. "On guard," I say. We draw towards one another, meet steely eye with steely eye, testing each other's nerve. My opponent's determination is strong and her movements hard to predict. I have the reach advantage but she has speed. Suddenly, a wild and savage attack that I am powerless to stop comes at me. Lilly wields her plastic light saber with crazy abandon, and I am easily defeated. "You win. You win. I give. I give," I say cowering behind the couch.

"C'mon, Auntie Em, you have to fight back. You won't be able to defeat The Empire with moves like that."

"You're right. I have to practice more," I say. Lilly strides off, acting the part of disapproving but well-meaning master, my little malcriada. She calls me Auntie Em, which makes me laugh. No one would confuse me with the sweet older woman in *The Wizard of Oz*, but I clicked my heels three times and appeared like magic back on the east coast—the place I still call home in my deepest heart—in order to be closer to Gilga and Lilly. The more time I spend with this little girl, the harder it is for me to be anywhere else. With nothing keeping me in Chicago at the moment, I moved temporarily to help Gilga raise her daughter. Gilga is out on a date and I am babysitting.

I can't remember if she is out with the Woman Who Is Afraid of Time or with yet another Boy Who Doesn't Know—some bartender she met while waiting for the aforementioned temporally-challenged woman. Her heart isn't really in it, but she will not be daunted. She says she needs to relearn everything from the bottom up, so she attacks dating with her usual grim, efficient determination, like back in our band days. Gomez quit his job and decided to follow Manny to California. Manny told us, somewhat dubiously, Gomez was spending all of his time writing again rather than looking for a new job. Manny makes enough for the two of them to live on, he says, but I could tell he was worried about Gomez. But then Gomez goes and surprises us all when the play he'd been working on gets picked up by a small theater in L.A. It is about a little girl named Melinda who falls beneath the ice and returns to her family with the soul of another little girl inside her, a soul that has been waiting at the lake bottom for a new body to fall so she could live again above the ice. He calls it *Frost Heaves Melinda.* Manny says it is terrifying and never wants to see it again, but he says it with so much pride that Gomez takes it as a compliment. And it is a compliment between two people who both went under and came back up, ghosts dying once again into life.

We, As Malcriadas, are come to claim our own, and that is you and that is we. It is Gilga who became a Mesopotamian prince and failed to conquer sleep. It is Francisco Gomes, who is also Gomez Addams, following the clipped and barbed rose stems back to his beloved. And it is Manny, whose name came back burning and sealed in a block of ice. And there is me, the daughter of a monster perched with talon and beak, whose shadow doesn't ever fit quite right. This could be an exaggeration; it could be a lie so much trickier than truth, but it isn't. It isn't a lie. We, As Malcriadas, are without guile, took names too big for our bodies hoping to convince ourselves and each other that we could hold out against the future; we took names too small for our bodies, names for fearsome things we pretended to have power over—a past that skulked by when it was least looked for. It was not enough. We wanted more—no matter how we fought it—and, unsurprisingly, ended with less. And yet, here we are—together again—at the sword point of middle age unsure where to go next and if we should go it alone or together to chase the names blowing by. Is this how they whisper? Like this? Like a first kiss that blooms and then browns? Or is it, like this? Like a common weed which only grows with other weeds?

CARLO MATOS is a bisexual+ writer who has published eleven books, including *We Prefer the Damned* (Unbound Edition Press) and *The Quitters* (Tortoise Books). His poems, stories, essays, and reviews have appeared in such journals as *Iowa Review, Rhino, DMQ Review*, and *Hobart*, among many others. Carlo has received grants and fellowships from Disquiet International Literary Program (Portugal), CantoMundo, the Illinois Arts Council, the Sundress Academy for the Arts, and the La Romita School of Art (Italy). He is also a founding member of the Portuguese-American writers collective Kale Soup for the Soul. His work has won the Heartland Poetry Prize and been nominated for a Pushcart and several Best of the Nets. He currently lives in Chicago, is a professor at the City Colleges of Chicago, and is a former MMA fighter and fencer. Follow him on Twitter @CarloMatos46. He blogs at carlomatos.blogspot.com.